We strip of
hurling the s
bin.

You get used to shared changing rooms early in your training, so we're as unselfconscious about being in the same room in our underwear as kids in kindergarten.

Until our arms collide mid-throw—and we both stop. I stop because the unexpected physical contact affects me in the way this man's been affecting me since the first handshake.

I don't know why he stops until he turns, grips my shoulders, tugs me close and kisses me.

Hard, hot, angry, almost, but oh, if his hands have zapping power, it's nothing to what his lips can do...

Dear Reader

I didn't feel it would be right to round off *Doctors in the Outback*, this series of four books set in the Australian Outback, without including one of the unique services operating in Queensland. Although Bilbarra doesn't exist, and the Flying O and G service depicted in this book is purely fictional, there *is* such a service operating in Queensland. It is based in Roma, where the Flying Surgeon is also based, and is funded by the Queensland Department of Health. The FOG— or Flying Gynae, as he is known—conducts regular clinics in rural and remote towns as well as being on call for obstetric or gynaecological emergencies. Through this service women of the Outback are able to access services which were once only available to their city cousins.

I am really enjoying my new life in the Outback, and I hope these books will bring you a taste of it—a taste of the variety of life in the bush, the highs and lows, the tears and laughter, and, of course, the love those that live out here seek and find.

With best wishes

Meredith Webber

Recent titles by the same author:

OUTBACK ENCOUNTER
OUTBACK MARRIAGE
OUTBACK ENGAGEMENT

DOCTORS
IN FLIGHT

BY
MEREDITH WEBBER

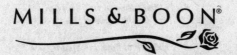

First published in Great Britain 2004
Harlequin Mills & Boon Limited,
Eton House, 18-24 Paradise Road, Richmond, Surrey TW9 1SR

© Meredith Webber 2004

ISBN 0 263 83883 8

Set in Times Roman 10½ on 12 pt.
03-0304-50441

Printed and bound in Spain
by Litografía Rosés, S.A., Barcelona

CHAPTER ONE

THEY can deny it all they like—sexism in the medical profession—but honestly, when you're one of four O and G registrars in a major hospital, three of whom have a Y chromosome, you know darned well why the one with two Xs ends up in Woop Woop.

'Send the woman,' someone says, and the—mostly male—powers that be all nod, delighted by the ease of the decision.

So though I'm not in any way a rampant feminist, I'm still seething about this 'arbitrary' selection when I arrive in Bilbarra. I don't think Woop Woop actually exists. It's just a name most people use when talking about the underpopulated regions of Australia—known colloquially as 'the outback' or, more simply 'the bush'. The fact that, umpteen years ago, I shot off to university to escape the bush and now here I am, boomeranged back to it, hasn't helped my mood any either.

Stepping off the plane onto tarmac hot enough to fry eggs, I'm hit by heavy, eucalypt-scented air, so dry I can feel my hair frizzing against my scalp. Actually, it smells good—the air, not my frizzing hair—but I'm not going to be seduced by the smell of an unpolluted atmosphere. I'm not that easy!

'Dr Green. Will Dr Green please report to the check-in desk.'

The message assaults my ears as soon as I scuttle thankfully into the air-conditioning in the small airport building.

The check-in desk?

Hallelujah, maybe someone's realised I'm all wrong for this job. I'm being sent back to the city!

I sashay across to the white counter on the right, pushing past a rather portly young man who's lurking beside it.

'I'm Dr Green.'

The official behind the desk looks startled—perhaps I sounded too enthusiastic about being me—and nods towards the portly gent, who's doing a stunned mullet imitation beside me.

'*You're* Dr Green?'

An alien would have been greeted with less disbelief.

'You have a problem with that?' I snap the words at him, the brief spurt of happiness replaced by ire now I realise I've been summoned to the check-in desk not to collect a ticket back to the city but so this guy can identify me.

'No, not me! Certainly not.' He holds up his hands as if to ward me off. Perhaps I sounded just a smidgen too aggressive. 'I'm Michael Reynolds, Dr Prentice's anaesthetist. He asked me to meet you—couldn't make it himself.'

He offers his right hand tentatively—no doubt wondering if I'll bite it or shake it—all the while staring at me so I begin to wonder if my hair did frizz right off my head when I hit the heat outside.

I shake his hand, which is soft and a bit clammy, but resist the urge to wipe my palm on my skirt when I'm done.

'Hillary Green,' I say. Even in the bush we're taught good manners. 'I'm looking forward to working with you and Dr Prentice.'

He gives me another disbelieving look, but he's obviously been brought up with manners, too, and as he ushers me towards the door, where a small tractor has pulled a trailer-load of luggage from the plane, he says politely, 'Hillary. That's an unusual name. Are you called Hilly?'

'Only by people brave enough to risk disembowelment or castration.'

OK, I come on a little strong at times, but a lifetime of being Silly Hilly or Hilly Dilly is enough to try a saint's patience.

'Yes, I see,' Michael mutters, taking the suitcase I've lifted off the trailer and heading towards the exit. 'The car's out this way.'

'Hey, that's not all,' I yell after him, but he's already gone. Muttering now myself, I lift off the other three cases and the box of books and another box with some kitchen things in it—try finding cardamom pods or Godiva chocolate, eaten only during those very special emergencies, in a country supermarket. I stand beside the pile until Michael returns.

'Good grief!' He's still muttering and throwing me strange looks, but he grabs the box of books and heads back out again. I follow, wheeling the two big cases, and we repeat the trek to collect the last one and the kitchen stuff.

'I should have brought a removal van,' he says when it's finally packed into the back of his roomy four-wheel-drive. Though he's carrying on about the luggage, I can't help feeling there's something else behind the looks and muttering.

A foreboding that has nothing to do with being back in the bush shivers along my nerves.

Michael does the tourist guide thing on the drive to town, pointing out the shooting club—like I'll be spending spare time there!—and the sewage farm—ditto—and finally the sale yards.

'It's sale day,' he adds unnecessarily as the aroma of the secretions of milling, agitated cattle seeps through the air-conditioning ducts and confirms, hey, I'm back in the bush.

'The boss's at the sales.'

'Cattle sales on a Sunday?'

'It's something special,' Michael says, as if the selling of cattle is a subject way beyond his comprehension. 'To do with bulls, I think. All I know is the boss had to go.'

He says this as if it's a good thing, and I'm about to ask why when he pulls up outside the hospital.

'Wow!'

Michael smiles properly for the first time since we met.

'Yeah, it's great, isn't it? The patient wings are all new but they married in bits of the old hospital as well. It takes a while to find your way around, but the place really works.'

He sounds so genuinely enthusiastic I forgive his earlier lapses.

'They're putting you up in the old nurses' quarters around the back, though once you have a look around the town you might decide to rent a place. That's if you can find one.'

We drive around the side of the modern, teal and gold and dull blue painted building and he stops again outside a tired wooden structure with glass louvres all down one side. None of the bright new paint was wasted out here.

'It's not much but no one else uses it so you'll have plenty of space to spread out.'

He's sounding so apologetic I start to worry again. With good reason, as it turns out. 'Not much' has to be the understatement of the year. The building consists of ten small single rooms—small? I kid you not! Nuns' cells would be bigger—opening off a long louvred veranda. A similarly louvred veranda runs along the back of the rooms. At the far end of the front veranda is an open space with a small rickety table, four ancient chairs, two lounge chairs and a television on a stand. Around the corner is a counter with a kitchen sink, and opposite it a stove that might have been new when the war ended—the First World War, that is.

Real windows replace the louvres at this end, and although at one time they had obviously had attractive coloured and patterned glass in them, some of the panes must have been broken over time and been replaced with clear glass, so the impression is of something patched together for expediency rather than looks.

Beyond this dreary living-kitchen area are two small rooms, which I assume contain essential plumbing fixtures.

'This is it?' I ask Michael, sure he must be joking.

'It's the only temporary accommodation the hospital has,' he says, then foolishly adds, 'Right now.'

I let it pass, though I know the FOG's anaesthetic registrars, like his O and G registrars, are sent up on a six-month rotation, and I guess he's in far superior temporary accommodation somewhere in the area. Did I tell you about the FOG? That's why I'm here, and while Michael's carting in the luggage—I told you I wasn't a rampant feminist—I'll fill you in.

The FOG is the Flying Obstetrician and Gynaecologist. The first service of this kind was started in Roma in southwest Queensland, and now there's also one here in Bilbarra, which is a large country town in Central Queensland. But 'based' means just that. The FOG holds regular consultancy sessions and operates in hospitals all over the place. The state government funds the O and G specialist, a plane, two pilots, an anaesthetist and an O and G registrar—who, for the moment for the Bilbarra service, is me.

Michael struggles along the veranda with the book box and one of the suitcases, while behind him a woman in dark blue calf-length trousers and a blue and white checked shirt tows a couple more suitcases.

'I can't believe they've sent a woman,' she says, abandoning the suitcases by the door of one of the cells and giving me a look that adds, And one who can't cart her own luggage at that!

I ignore the unspoken criticism, but am moved to protest about the disbelief statement. First acquaintance with my temporary abode hasn't improved my temper any.

'What is it with you people? You can't be antediluvian enough to think women should be kept barefoot and pregnant and living on the outskirts of town.'

'It's not us you have to worry about, sweetie,' the woman snaps. 'It's the boss. And though not exactly antediluvian, he sure hates working with female registrars.'

I am about to launch into my tirade about sexism in the medical profession when I realise it will be wasted on this audience. I'll keep it for 'the boss' himself and, boy, will I enjoy letting loose on him!

'Well, tough buns,' I tell the newcomer, then, remembering my manners for the second time since my arrival, shove out my hand.

'I'm Hillary Green.'

'And don't call her Hilly,' Michael adds, then beats a strategic retreat, no doubt preferring lugging luggage to being in the firing line should war break out between us.

The woman steps forward.

'Maureen Sharp. I'm acting Director Of Nursing. Also

Theatre sister when the boss operates in Bilbarra. I suppose you know he has a small private practice here as well as his other work.'

I shake her hand, but my brain's working overtime.

Does Dr Prentice not have a first name? I know he has initials—G.R.—they're on the letter I received telling me to report to him.

Or does he not allow underlings to use his first name, hence this almost reverent use of 'the boss'?

Not that his name's the issue here—

'Why doesn't he like working with female registrars?'

Maureen shrugs her ample shoulders.

'Who knows? I haven't been here long myself but it seems to be general knowledge. Perhaps he had a bad experience some time? He's not exactly chatty, the boss, or forthcoming about his thoughts and feelings. Damn good doctor, though. And caring in an odd, detached kind of way.'

Maureen stops, as if afraid she'd said too much, and looks around.

'This place is a dump but there's not much else available at the moment. There's a new mine being opened in the area and all available accommodation's been snapped up by the mining company. Even then, there's not enough to house the influx and the caravan park's full as well.'

She turns to watch Michael approach with yet more luggage, and smiles one of those infuriatingly smug, poor-silly-you smiles.

'Think you'll get to wear all that gear while you're here?'

I don't deign to explain that, owing to an inbred miserliness, I've given up my flat and, as you might guess, I refuse to spend money on storage for my possessions. Everything I own is packed into those cases and boxes.

'Come across to the hospital when you're settled in. I'll introduce you to Georgia, the boss's secretary. She's come in today to catch up on some paperwork because she's going on leave from tomorrow. She's offered to take you over the hospital, show you the dining room where you can get your meals if you want hospital food, fix you up with a cell phone and pager and your duty roster. You did bring an alarm clock?'

She glances towards the stack of luggage, and though I've never owned an alarm clock in my life I lie and say of course I have.

I know what you're thinking, but it isn't because of my Scrooge streak that I don't own an alarm clock. I happen to be blessed with a very reliable internal alarm. I tell it what time I need to wake up, and it works every time.

Maureen has departed by now. Michael has delivered all the luggage and is hovering, as if uncertain what he should do next.

'The boss said he'd be back by two and he'll see you then.'

Said boss's sidekick looks so uncomfortable I feel sorry for him.

'Don't worry about it,' I say. 'So, I'm a woman. What's the worst this ogre can do? Perform a sex-change op? A bit drastic, surely. Send me back? Hell, I wouldn't fight him on that score. Do you think I wanted to come out and languish in this backwater for six months, dropping out of the sky to deliver a baby like some new-age stork?'

'Actually, you'll spend more time operating on gynaecological problems,' a deep voice says. 'We do very few regular deliveries.'

I spin around to see a tall, dark-haired, strong-featured man with glasses striding down the veranda.

Soundlessly?

MEREDITH WEBBER

13

I look down at his feet and see the socks, recognising immediately the country habit of kicking off outside shoes at the front door.

He must have seen my eyes drop for he adds, 'I've been at the sale yards and, though this place is no Hilton, there's no point in making it worse by tramping manure through it.'

He stops about a metre in front of me.

'Dr H Green, I presume?'

'Dr GR Prentice?' I counter, looking challengingly up at him, seeing the glint of grey eyes behind the lenses of his glasses—grey eyes that are disconcertingly soft.

'G—Richard,' he says, so quietly I miss the first bit.

He shoots out his hand and it would be churlish not to shake it, but within seconds of my skin meeting his I realise churlish would have been better.

Much better!

The man must have had some kind of static electricity overload because even that casual touch sends a buzzing sensation along my nerves. And by the time I've conquered that sensation, it's too late to ask him to repeat his first name.

'Hillary!' I manage to blurt out, removing my hand from the danger zone and checking to see how badly scorched the skin is.

Not a sign of redness, but I'm still tingly enough to know I didn't imagine the voltage passing through me.

'Did you do that?' he asks, peering down at me through the glasses.

'Do what?' I ask, certain my body hasn't been guilty of any socially unacceptable act in the couple of seconds he's been near me.

He ignores me answering his question with a question and turns his attention to the pile of luggage.

'You know you're only temporary?'

Very temporary, I think, remembering what I was saying as he crept up behind us, but I'm not going to bite.

'Yes.'

He turns back to study me, as if surprised I'm not offering more, but my mouth has got me into trouble often enough for me to learn when to keep it closed.

Most of the time...

Michael has moved away and is opening louvres along the veranda. A slight breeze drifts in, carrying a waft of cattle-yard scent from the new arrival to me. Redolent of all I fled when I headed for the city, I should be repulsed but, damn it all, I feel tears smarting in my eyes as it washes across me, and for an instant I want to be a child again, casting myself into my grandfather's arms when he comes in from a day's work.

However, given both the buzzing and this man's apparent aversion to women, casting myself into his arms isn't an option. Casting myself into *any* man's arms isn't an option! I'm a woman with her hormones under control. That buzzing thing is nothing more than a temporary glitch.

He's moved on anyway, rounding the corner to talk to Michael.

'Gilgudgel has a young woman, protracted labour and the descent's stopped. It's a good opportunity to show Dr Green how we work so we'll all go. Dave's fuelling the plane now.'

He reappears, striding back down the veranda in his stockinged feet.

'Come on, Blue!' he throws over his shoulder. 'We've got work to do.'

When you're born with hair the colour of a rusty watertank, you might start life fighting people who call you

Blue—especially when your surname's Green and Blue
Green sounds like a name invented for a country music
singer or a stand-up comedian—but it's a losing battle, so
I just follow, thinking it would have been nice to check
out the bathroom facilities.

'You can use the bathroom at the airport.'

He's standing at the bottom of the steps by now, pulling
on worn elastic-sided boots. Tall, lanky, a bit dusty from
the sale yards, black hair with a few gleams of silver
where the sun catches it, straight thinnish nose propping
up the silver-rimmed glasses, good chin. Not your average, everyday mind-reader.

'Do I need to take anything?'

He raises an eyebrow as Michael slides past us and
heads for his car.

'Your stethoscope if you prefer to use your own, but
apart from that just yourself. We're quite civilised out
here, Blue. Gilgudgel is an old hospital but it's well main-
tained and stocked. There's no point in having this service, or the flying surgeon, if the hospitals don't have up-
to-date equipment we can use.'

My stethoscope—where did I pack it? Glancing at the
pile of luggage doesn't help in any way and I can't see
GR waiting while I unpack the lot.

Do I really need it, apart from using it as a prop to
make me look like a doctor rather than the cleaner?

Uncertainty makes my stomach churn so I forget the
thing and hurry to catch up with the boss.

He's headed towards a dusty Range Rover pulled in
beside Michael's car. Determined not to trot along at his
heels, I take a couple of huge strides to catch up and, it
being the kind of day it is, trip over an uneven edge on
the concrete path.

I have to give him full marks for reaction. His hand

whips out and grabs my arm, saving me from landing face down on the path.

'Steady on. The hospital can't afford compensation claims, though I suppose if you'd broken something I could have sent you back.'

'I could try again,' I snap, wanting to shake his hand off my arm before the buzzing sensation drives me mad. 'What kind of a break would you like? Wrist, arm, shoulder? Do you have any preferences?'

His snort of laughter sends the pink and grey galahs, feeding on grass seed in the hospital lawn, swirling into the air, but at least he drops my arm—so quickly I nearly fall again.

'A temper to go with the hair, eh, Blue?' He's grinning now, apparently delighted to discover this very small character flaw.

'Only when provoked,' I tell him, as he opens the car door for me.

I edge past him, catching again that strange evocative scent of man and dust and sweat and cattle, glancing up involuntarily to make sure it *isn't* my grandfather, though it would have had to be reincarnation—Granddad having been dead these many years.

G— Richard Prentice makes an unlikely angel, I decide as I watch his progress around the bonnet of the vehicle. With his thin, dark face, he'd be closer to a devil. I picture a couple of small horns sprouting from his head and am smiling at the image when he climbs in beside me.

'Gilgudgel is about forty-five minutes' flying time from Bilbarra. It's an eight-bed hospital, staffed by half a dozen local RNs and some agency nurses working on contract. The medical superintendent was injured in a car accident four weeks ago and hasn't been replaced, although there's talk of a locum coming next week.'

He's telling me this while driving through town at a pace that makes me wonder if there's a higher than average motor vehicle accident rate among outback medicos. I cling to the prayer bar and make promises to God. If I get out of it alive, I'll phone Gran and tell her I love her. First thing! Before anything else, even using the bathroom at the airport.

We reach the airport and, of course, I head straight to the bathroom, and when I finish with necessities I splash my face with water and run my wet hands through my hair. I'm quite proud of my hair as it represents the single greatest economy I've ever discovered. It curls, you see, as well as being red, so I used to spend a fortune at the hairdresser trying to tame it.

Then the 'Shave for a Cure' idea came in. You know, a fundraising idea where you promise you'll get your head shaved if people give you money, and the funds go to the Leukaemia Foundation. Well, the big hospitals all have a mammoth effort each year, and usually get a noted hairdresser or TV star to do the shaving. All I need to do is collect money from doubting colleagues, then line up for a shave while those same colleagues hoot and whistle. I'm then bald, which is a minor irritant for a month or so, but everyone understands it's for a great cause, and my skull's a good shape. Then my hair starts to grow back. Right now, a couple of months post-shave, it's the perfect wash-and-wear length, about an inch and a half long all over. By the time it's so unruly it *really* needs attention, the twelve months are up and I line up again.

I must have been a little longer congratulating myself than I realised because I emerge to find GR Prentice waiting right outside the door.

'You told me to go,' I remind him, embarrassment vying with anger. 'And the foot-tapping routine is superfluous. Your facial expression shows enough impatience for me to get the message.'

He ignores me, again leading me at a furious clip through the deserted terminal and back out into the eucalypt-scented air.

Which has grown hotter!

'That's our plane.'

He points to a shiny silver aircraft with a state badge on the side, and waves his hand to indicate the middle-aged man standing by the nose.

'And that's Dave over there with Michael. Dave's one of two pilots we use. Dave, Blue—Blue, Dave.'

I'm about to tell Dave I've got a real name, and perhaps warn him about shortening it, when I glance at GR and realise that's exactly what he's waiting for me to do.

So's Michael.

I clamp my lips shut, tilt my head in a superior fashion and climb into the plane, taking the seat behind the pilot's.

She's a little beauty. A four-seater Cessna, workhorse of the west. Touching the hot vinyl on the seats, smelling the avgas, I wonder if I made the wrong decision, going into medicine instead of the air force. The never-fading thrill of delivering a healthy newborn baby instead of living with the adrenaline rush of flight.

Not that an O and G's job doesn't have its own adrenaline rush…

Michael gets in next and settles beside me, putting on his harness then pulling a book out of the pocket between the seats. He's making it very clear he has no intention of talking to me on this jaunt. In case it puts him offside with the boss?

Could he really be that weak?

'You comfortable back there?'

The man they call 'the boss' hasn't asked because he

wants to know—I can tell that from his voice—so I guess he's trying to remind me of my place in the scheme of things—my unimportance.

Don't goad him, I remind myself, but I've never listened—not to me or anyone else.

'What'll you do if I say no? Shift back here and let me have the window seat?'

'You've got a window,' he points out, and turns away, adjusting his harness, ignoring me so pointedly I want to stick out my tongue and waggle my fingers in my ears, pulling childish faces at his back.

I don't, you'll be pleased to hear. I'm not *that* childish! But I do strap myself in, then I lean back and close my eyes, trying to work out why the man is irritating me so much.

Because I was forewarned he doesn't like working with women? Is that why I feel compelled to get in first with the smart comments?

Or are my smart comments an automatic reaction to the buzz? A form of self-protection?

I'm wondering why he doesn't like working with women—mainly to avoid thinking about the buzz—as the plane taxis forward, picks up speed, then lifts like a bird into the air.

'Frightened? Never been in a small plane?'

He's not only interrupting my train of thought, but the hand he's rested—very briefly—on my knee when he turned again is zapping me.

'I've *flown* planes bigger than this,' I tell him, shifting my knee although he's already lifted his hand. However, it's still hovering in the general direction of my left leg so I shift a bit more to be certain I'm out of range. 'I was thinking about the patient—about work.'

'And?' he prompts.

'How much do you know? Enough to assume we'll have to do a Caesar? And, if so, do you have a preference for anaesthetising patients for it? Epidural or a light anaesthesia?'

'Epidural every time. Most women who've opted for normal birth are stressed by not being able to deliver normally. At least seeing the baby at the earliest possible moment is some comfort to them.'

So he behaves better towards his patients than he does towards his staff! Although that isn't entirely fair. He's been punctiliously polite to me. I know I should be pleased about his attitude to patients, but when I decide to not like someone I'd prefer them to be unlikable all the way through. Not that I share this thought with GR.

In fact, I close my eyes again and lean my head back against the head-rest, though this time not to think but to shut out the man who is still turned towards me, studying me as if a closer inspection might change me into something more acceptable—like a man!

We land, smoothly, at an airport not much bigger than a cow paddock, and as we taxi to a halt, a white station wagon pulls up beside the plane. The woman driver greets GR with a hug—so it isn't all women he's against—and shakes hands with Michael, who is very quiet and looking a bit green. Then, as I clamber down, she comes forward.

'I'm Callie, duty sister. Gregor tells me you'd just arrived when he whisked you away. Sorry about that, but it's a first baby and she's been in labour, as far as we can make out, for eighteen hours and is just about exhausted.'

So, his name's Gregor—unusual but nice—but before I can dwell on whether I'll ever be allowed to use it, something else strikes me.

'As far as you can make out?'

Callie ushers me into the car.

'Hope you don't mind the back seat—the boss's legs just don't fit if I put him in there.'

She shuts the door and goes around to get in behind the wheel, while 'the boss' climbs in and sits in front of me—great view of back of male neck and hair in need of a trim. Michael gets in on the other side, puts on his seat belt then rests his head against the window.

No one says anything so I guess this behaviour is normal for Michael.

'She's on the road with her husband,' Callie adds. 'They've got cattle in the long paddock.' She turns as she pulls on her seat belt. 'You know about the long paddock?'

Do I ever! I spent one entire Christmas holiday—that's two months—riding herd on a mob of breeding cows and calves as Granddad drove them down the grass verges of outback roads, finding enough feed to keep them alive when the paddocks back home were bare.

'How long have they been on the road?'

Callie smiles at me in the rear-view mirror.

'As far as I can make out, right through the pregnancy. Out here we talk about kids born in the saddle—well, this one was practically conceived in it as well.'

Gregor Richard hasn't offered any comment, which is OK with me. If he's not talking, he won't be stirring me up.

That's not entirely true. It must be the electricity overload he carries because, just sitting there, he's stirring me up. I can't believe this is happening. Not now. Not here! Not at my age.

In case you're wondering, I'm twenty-seven and you'd assume I'd be well passed the danger age of being a hostage to my hormones. Actually, I spent most of my adolescent and adult years making damn sure I wasn't *ever* going to be hostage to my hormones!

I turn to Michael, but he's peering desperately out the window on his side, and a suspicion that all is not well with him finally begins to form in my head.

Travel sickness? And he's working in a position that has him travelling four days out of five? Does he throw up on a rough flight?

I decide I'm glad GR has taken the front seat in the car focus all my attention on the view beyond the window.

Gilgudgel looks just like most small country towns I've visited, but once again the hospital is a surprise. Despite the fact the countryside around the town is parched and dry, the hospital is surrounded by brilliant green grass, while a scattering of large shade trees makes the area look like parkland.

'The hospital has its own bore. Before a dam was built five years ago, the whole town relied on bore water,' Callie explains. 'Terrible to shower in—your hair always smells.'

'Rotten egg gas!' I say sympathetically, and she laughs. 'You've been here before.'

'Used bore water, anyway,' I tell her, but the boss and Michael are already out of the car and disappearing into the hospital. With a sigh, I follow, tiredness from last-minute packing the previous night, plus two flights and a load of sensory stuff I could live without, making every step an effort.

I must be sighing, or maybe whining quietly to myself, because Callie says, 'I don't know why he dragged you along, given that you've just arrived.'

'I think he decided to throw me in at the deep end— probably in the hope I couldn't swim,' I mutter at her as we push through the front door, and, of course, GR has stopped to ask her something so he catches my bit of the conversation.

'Can you?' he asks, dark eyebrow rising.

'You'd better believe it!' I tell him, then we continue on our not-so-merry way.

The patient is a thin slip of a woman, so small the bulge of her stomach seems to have taken over her body like an alien force. She is pale and sweaty, but the young man by her side, clinging tightly to her hand, looks far more worn out.

'This is Wendy, and her husband Paul,' Callie says, and GR settles himself on the other side of the woman and takes her hand. He talks quietly to her for a moment, then introduces me.

'Dr Green has just arrived from the Royal Women's and has all the latest training and information. You couldn't be in better hands.'

I shake Wendy's hand, listening to Callie as she reads out the details of Wendy's labour, the slow dilatation of the cervix in spite of increasingly close contractions, then the cessation of all activity in spite of drugs which would normally encourage it.

I spread my palm on Wendy's belly and press gently, feeling for the position of the baby through the taut skin.

'Wendy's been here eight hours,' Callie says. 'At first everything went well, although the descent has been very slow. It had stopped completely when I phoned you.'

She passes me the chart, and I check the drugs that have been given, then I look at Gregor.

'Your decision,' he says.

'I'd do a Caesar,' I reply. 'Right now, before Wendy suffers any more pain. And though I'd love to show you just how good I am, I was up most of last night cleaning

out my flat, then left for the airport very early this morning. As I don't officially start work here until tomorrow,
I think you should do it.'

OK, so I've probably blown it, pushing the op onto him
when he's obviously brought me with him so I can do it
and he can judge my competence, but this is the life of
two people we're talking about here—Wendy's and her
unborn baby's—and though I've operated tired before,
why do it when there's a wide-awake, full-blown specialist available?

The silence in the room can't last more than a couple
of seconds, but it feels like a lifetime to me. Then GR
smiles, not a whole smile but a funny little quirk of lips
on one side of his mouth.

'Good judgement call, Blue,' he says, then turns to
Callie, giving directions for Wendy to be wheeled into the
OR.

Relieved—even a wee bit flattered—but uncertain what
to do next, I explain to Paul what's going to happen and
why.

'I should think they'll let you stand in there with
Wendy,' I add. 'Just give them time to get her ready.'

He doesn't seem overjoyed at the prospect of watching
a surgeon slit his wife's belly open so to take his mind
off it, I ask him about the cattle.

'Is there someone with them or have you had to yard
them?'

'We've got an electric fence around them. My dad's
there, and the dogs, but you can't move them on with
only one person. He's got the horses and the truck. He'll
just stay where he is until this is over.'

I can imagine the scene, inch-wide plastic tape with a
conductive wire running through it strung on pegs along
the road, the ends connected to a battery which feeds a

charge through it. Paul's father, watching the cattle, anxious lest a calf get under the tape, anxious, too, no doubt, about his daughter-in-law.

'And then?' I ask, and Paul shrugs.

'Wendy says it will be OK. She'll take over the truck and Dad and I'll do the riding for a few weeks.'

'OK, Blue, you can bring the father-to-be in if he wants to come. Make sure he's gowned.'

Gregor's order reminds me I'm a doctor, not a cattle-drover.

'You OK with this? Do you want to go in there?' I ask Paul, and he swallows then nods.

'Reckon I've seen worse with cattle,' he says, and gamely accompanies me as I head in the direction the others took, finding a small changing room and a gown, mask and slippers for the two of us.

Michael's asking Wendy about allergies as we come in, then he explains about the drug he'll use and how she'll need to lie on her side so he can insert the needle into the space around the fibrous outer covering of the spinal cord.

It's all systems go. Michael has regained some colour in his face and is working swiftly and competently—the theatre is an anaesthetist's domain, although most surgeons think it's theirs. He helps Wendy roll onto her side and inserts the needle, effectively blocking off all sensation to the parts of her body below her waist.

As she rolls back, a theatre nurse, whose ID is lost somewhere under her theatre pyjamas, swabs her belly, then spreads drapes around the area where GR will make his incision. Callie then helps her erect a drape so the woozy Wendy doesn't have to see the whole op in gory detail. Saves Paul watching it, too.

But I move away from Paul so I can watch because, for me, every time a new baby is lifted into the world, the thrill is indescribable.

CHAPTER TWO

WENDY is sutured up, then transferred to a single-bed ward, the tiny baby boy in a crib beside her. I trail along behind, fascinated as ever by the miracle of a newborn infant, bending over the crib, blinking back a tear as his tiny hand fists around my finger. Then a 'hrmph' of a cough alerts me to the fact the boss is waiting.

Back to the plane. The boss is obviously not a man who hangs around praising the parents or admiring their joint production.

Fair enough, I can handle that. In fact, it's a good thing as my soppiness over babies seems to be getting worse rather than better with exposure. I refuse to believe it's to do with ticking clocks…

We clamber aboard. Note to self—always wear trousers of some kind. The person who invented miniskirts didn't think about the wearer having to get in and out of small planes. Michael buries his head in his book and Dave takes us up, smooth and easy. Gregor waits until we level out, then turns to me.

'Tomorrow we go to Creamunna and Grandchester. You and I run in tandem—one in Theatre and one consulting. Tomorrow you'll do the consulting and I'll do the ops.'

'Is that how you normally work?' I only ask because he's obviously explaining this for my benefit so the least I can do is show an interest. Besides, thinking about work stops me thinking about other things—like the effect he has on me.

'Not all the time. In fact, I do a lot of the consulting because I like to give my registrars the opportunity for as much surgical work as possible.'

'So why are we swapping roles tomorrow?'

Can't help myself, can I?

'Because the patients you see tomorrow will be the ones you'll operate on the next time we visit those towns—which in these two towns will be in a month,' he responds, frowning as if to impress on me that this is serious stuff. 'I work this way whenever a new registrar starts so at least your first lot of surgical patients will have met you before they see you in Theatre.'

'Surely all consults don't lead to Theatre? Don't some patients have non-surgical problems?'

'The majority of non-surgical things can be handled by the local GP,' he explains, 'but you'll be seeing post-op patients in each town, as well as consulting with those who have problems that need surgery. Michael and I, meanwhile, will be doing one or maybe two ops—three or four if they're minor.'

'What kind of surgery can you do?'

He leans a little closer towards me and frowns as if he doesn't understand the question.

'Most gynaecological surgery, though I send cancer patients to a base hospital on the coast because they'll need ongoing treatment we can't provide. Apart from that, we do pretty much everything.'

'I was thinking of equipment. Would small country hospitals have laparoscopy equipment?'

'Some do, some don't. When the FOG service was extended, service clubs and other organisations in a lot of the towns we visit got together to raise money specifically for that one piece of equipment. Also, people are used to travelling long distances for medical services, so if they need an exploratory examination they're usually willing to go to a town that has the facilities. They're very adaptable—country people.'

Well, der! I want to say, but don't. See, I *can* hold my tongue at times! He doesn't appear to have anything further to say, so I turn to look out the window at the flat red-brown earth below the plane, seeing the dots that I know are stunted trees, the occasional hill poking up towards the sky.

But no scenery can diminish the man's presence in the close confines of the plane's cabin, and the earlier conversations about his dislike of women colleagues nibbles away beneath my skin like a burrowing insect.

So it's hardly surprising that, a couple of hours later, I blurt out the question that's bugging me. Really blurt it out...

I'm sitting in his office at the hospital, studying the schedule presented to me by Georgia. I'm actually sitting in what I assume is his chair, behind what I know is his desk, but only because I needed to spread out the map Georgia has given me with the schedules, and this is the only clear space I can find.

'Comfy?' he says, entering so quietly I don't hear him, though he's definitely wearing shoes this time.

I leap about six inches into the air and, being caught in the wrong, go straight on the attack.

'Why don't you like women registrars?'

The dark face stills for a moment, then his lips do the quirky thing that might almost be a smile if you are fast enough to catch it.

'I have nothing against women registrars in general,' he tells me, dropping into one of the visitors' chairs on the other side of his desk. 'In fact, I think women doctors do an excellent job.'

'Just not within spitting distance of you.'

I'm usually not this aggressive, but something about GR Prentice rattles my cage. Even when he's not touching me.

'Just not in remote areas,' he says, amending my words. 'Or, to be more precise, not in O and G registrar positions in remote areas.'

'Heaven forbid you should be anything less than precise,' I mutter, then wade into the argument again. 'Do you have a reason for this prejudice or is it simply a personal quirk on your part?'

A dark eyebrow rises.

'Do you speak to all your superiors this way?'

In other words, back off, Hillary! I know that's what he's saying, but I can't let it go.

'No, I don't, but it seems to me we'll make a more effective team if I understand where you're coming from on this subject. I mean, if it's something simple like you being allergic to perfume, I can assure you I don't wear it when I'm working because any number of patients could also have allergies.'

I try a smile. 'See, we've sorted that one out already.'

No answering smile, not even a lip quirk. Instead, he studies his watch as if it might tell him what to say next, then looks up at me.

'It's late, you haven't had time to unpack, let alone shop or order a meal from the kitchen. Why don't you pop over to your quarters, grab a quick shower, and I'll buy you dinner? There's a really good Chinese restaurant in town, an assortment of pubs that do food, or a steakhouse. You can take your pick, and we'll talk over dinner.'

This is where a real smart-mouth should come into her own, but do I have an answer? No way! I'm flummoxed, gob-smacked, bamboozled, flabbergasted—all of the above?—and I sit there like a big ninny, probably opening and closing my mouth in the manner of a dying fish. Not a pretty picture, I'm sure you'll agree.

'You'll have to go now if you want a shower before we eat,' he adds calmly. 'I like to be home by ten to watch the weekend sports round-up.'

I peer across his desk at him, certain he can't possibly be a reincarnation of my grandfather. There are probably a lot of men in the world who consider their life isn't complete without a final evening viewing of the weekend sports round-up programme.

'Go! Scat!' he says, standing up and making shooing movements towards the door. 'Quite apart from anything else, I need to get at my desk. I'll meet you at my car in fifteen minutes.'

I scat—or should that be skit? Scatter? He's certainly left my brain feeling scattered.

Back in the nurses' quarters, the boxes and suitcases are still in the same place—no good fairy has come and put things away for me. And I haven't rung Gran!

Well, the boss can wait a few extra minutes. I find my own mobile, not the work one, and press her preset number, at the same time hauling the case I'm pretty sure has clean clothes in it into one of the cells. With a single bed, wardrobe-dressing-table combination and chair already in there, the suitcase and I take up all the remaining space. No room to open it.

I drag it back out onto the veranda and open it there, digging through it for something cool and comfortable as the heat of the day still lingers. Ha! The long singlet dress which I love because it's a soft cotton knit and is comfy to wear, and if the dark green colour makes my eyes look greener, that's a bonus, isn't it? Pete loved it, too, I think because he could slide the straps off my shoulders and the whole thing would slip down to the floor. Ow! A brief spasm of pain for the loss of Pete.

Who's Pete, you ask? He's the man I really should have married—really thought I *would* marry, in fact. But things didn't turn out that way and right now—

A voice is yelling in my ear.

'Who's there? Who is it? Is that you, Hillary?'

'Yes, Gran. Sorry. I'm trying to unpack at the same time. They've put me in the old nurses' quarters here at Bilbarra and the rooms are so small I have to unpack on the veranda. Anyway, I'm just ringing to let you know I've arrived safe and sound.'

She can't possibly have heard the 'safe and sound' bit because she's talking again—positively shrieking down the phone.

'Bilbarra? You didn't tell me you were going to Bilbarra! You said ''way out Woop Woop'' but didn't mention Bilbarra.'

OK, so I didn't mention the name of the town! I lift the phone away from my ear and peer suspiciously at it as Gran's tirade continues. Now she's going on about the nurses' quarters. Does she think this a come-down for a doctor?

'It's only for six months so what does it matter, Gran?' I ask, when she pauses for breath.

'Of course it matters. I'll tell you when I get there. I'll leave in the morning.'

She hangs up before I can ask more questions, and as I am now down to ten minutes before I'm due to meet GR at the car, I can't phone her back.

Clutching the singlet dress and clean underwear in one hand and my toothbrush bag in the other, I head for the shower. I must be tireder than I realised—thinking Gran said she was coming to Bilbarra…

I make it in the allotted fifteen minutes, but only because I'm a minimal-care kind of person. I've lived in subtropical climates long enough to know make-up is a waste of time and effort, not to mention money. In this weather, it slides off the face almost as soon as it's applied, so why bother? I do the moisturising thing and darken my eyelashes with mascara—I'm a pale-skinned redhead and they need help!—then slide some lip-gloss over my lips, but that's it.

GR—I can't even *think* of him as Gregor yet—gives a nod, which I assume is an acknowledgment of my punctuality, then his gaze slides down the long lines of the singlet dress, coming to rest on my sandals for a moment, before returning to my face.

'The pavements out here can be rough,' he says—unmistakable disapproval of the three-inch heels on my footwear. But when you're five-five in a world that seems made up of giants, you do your best! 'You wouldn't want to turn an ankle.'

'Is that a cute way of reminding me I nearly fell over earlier?'

He looks surprised.

'Did you? I don't remember that. And I rarely do cute. I tend to say what I think and I was simply stating a fact. Where there are footpaths in Bilbarra, they are usually rough.'

I take in the footpath stuff, but I'm really thinking about the first part of his reply. Whatever he was doing to me— the electric zapping—must be totally unconscious, and definitely one-sided, or he'd remember grabbing my arm.

I slide past him—he's holding the door for me again, something the non-feminist part of me appreciates—and into the car, thinking about the dangers attached to the unconscious delivery of electrical impulses. The man should wear a warning sign.

'I hope you're as prompt first thing in the morning,' he says, as if the ankle-turning conversation had never happened.

'I will be,' I assure him.

He drives back to the centre of town, asking on the way about my eating preference.

That's a no-brainer.

'Chinese, but I should warn you, if you want to share meals, I'm a rice, noodles and veggies girl.'

'Good grief! A vegetarian in sheep and cattle country!'

'I am not a vegetarian, I'm simply telling you my food preferences in a Chinese restaurant.'

He gave a huff of either exasperation or disbelief—not an easy man to read—and climbs out of the car. I open the door and jump down before he gets around the bonnet, and am about to shut the door when he grabs it out of my hand.

'Don't slam it. It's aluminium. It buckles easily.'

For the second time in less than an hour the opportunity for a smart retort slips by me. GR is standing close enough for us to kiss, and his hand, zapping its potent power, is covering mine on the doorhandle. My breathing's gone wonky, and I'm sure my knees are going to give way any minute, while there's a slow sizzle of something I don't want to think about deep down in my abdomen.

Thoughts of Pete return—only this time I'm remembering his attempts to describe what happened to him when he met Claudia—and I regret I teased him. Though I only teased him because I had no idea of what he was talking about. I certainly hadn't experienced the same symptoms with him…

'You OK?'

GR has shut the door—gently—and is now peering down at me. I look up and see the neon sign of the restaurant's name—Li Min—flash first red, then yellow across his glasses.

'Must be tireder than I realised,' I mutter, and duck away from him, heading towards the restaurant and, hopefully, sanity.

'I wasn't going to kiss you.'

I must be hearing things. I turn to frown at him.

'*What* did you say?'

'I said I wasn't going to hit you. Out there. With the door. You flinched away.'

Thank heavens! He *didn't* read my mind. *Doesn't* know I'd had the weirdest sensation that his lips were about to close in on mine.

Though now I check his face—he's talking to a woman at the front desk—I wonder if the words he said the second time were a lie. Eyes hidden behind glasses are hard to read but there's a slight frown drawing the well-shaped dark eyebrows together, as if he's puzzled over something.

We're shown to a table, and a smiling young waitress asks about drinks. I opt for water, knowing alcohol in any form will send me straight to sleep. GR orders a light beer, then picks up his menu and studies it. I know what I'm having—vegetable sate and steamed rice—so I take the opportunity to study him.

The glasses give him a nerdy look, but mentally removing them doesn't make him a conventionally handsome man. Too intense, somehow.

The waitress returns with his beer and a flask of cold water, pouring me a glass. She then hovers, pad in hand, beside me so I order, GR orders, she disappears and silence reigns.

I know I should break it, but I'm suddenly too tired to care why the man doesn't like working with women registrars. I'm also feeling creeped out by the effect of his touch, and more than slightly confused, in the back part of my mind, by Gran's conversation. Surely God wouldn't land me with a nerve-zapping, woman-hating boss and Gran both at the same time. I have a sudden urge to put my head down on the table and have a little sleep.

'Try to stay awake long enough to eat,' GR says, and my head shoots up so quickly I'm surprised I haven't dislocated my neck. 'We don't have to talk but you should eat. We don't work long days—by which I mean we don't have a huge daily patient load—but the travelling's tiring until you get used to it.'

'I thought we came here to talk,' I remind him, knowing if I keep talking there's less chance I'll fall asleep in my noodles. 'About why you don't like working with women registrars.'

Trying to read some reaction in his face is like trying to fathom the emotions of the man in the moon. Bland, that's what he is.

And silent, now the question's out in the open again. But he doesn't seem uneasy—just as if silent is normal for him. I think back over the strange afternoon and realise the only times he spoke were to impart information about the job.

Apart from when he asked me to have dinner with him—though I guess that's about the job, too.

'Don't frown like that,' he says. 'It's not a fatal flaw in my character. I've just had a bad run with female registrars. I also happen to have mixed feelings about women specialising in O and G.'

Were they late for work—the ones he had a bad run with? I just finished thinking this when his second statement grabs my attention!

'Because they can't work with other women? Can't empathise with women's problems? I know it was a male domain for a long time, and this might come as a great shock to you, but I can assure you the vast majority of women would prefer to see another woman when it comes to problems with their private parts.'

The heads of other diners swivel in our direction and I realise my voice may have risen slightly at the end of the final sentence, but this man has the ability to stir me up without even trying.

'I know that,' he says mildly. 'Actually, it works both ways. The majority of men would prefer a fellow male checked them out for an inguinal hernia or a prostate problem.'

'I'd have thought some men wouldn't mind having a woman holding their testicles while they coughed,' I snipe, though I know exactly what he means. What I don't expect is for the fellow with his back to me at the next table to actually fall off his chair.

By the time GR has helped him to his feet, and glared at me as if it was my fault the idiot was tipping backwards to eavesdrop on our conversation, our meals have arrived. The delicate aromas start my taste-buds working overtime and I immediately lose all interest in GR Prentice's opinions on women O and G specialists.

CHAPTER THREE

WE EAT in silence that's companionable enough, by which I mean GR seems to appreciate food as much as I do.

'I have to admit defeat,' I say, pushing my bowl reluctantly away and eyeing the remaining vegetables on the serving plate with great regret. 'That was fantastic!'

'The food's always good,' GR responds, himself eyeing my leftovers.

'Help yourself,' I say, and finally win a smile.

'I thought you'd never offer. It's only that I've never ordered that particular dish but it looks and smells so good I've been dying to taste it.'

He scoops a small amount into his bowl and lifts a chopstick-load towards his lips.

Nice lips—full, without being pink or puffy the way some men's lips get. Not that I'm an expert on male lips—it's just that one notices these things.

'You could have tried it earlier. I did offer.' That's me distracting myself from his lips.

It doesn't work as he finishes the mouthful and smiles—a real smile this time that moves those full lips far enough to press a couple of brackets of wrinkles into his cheeks, and crinkle the skin at the corners of his eyes, and make the grey eyes gleam behind the glasses. Though, to be perfectly honest, I can't see their colour in the dim light of the restaurant, just the gleam.

'Take a single morsel away from you, when you fell on it as if you hadn't eaten for days?'

I realise he's talking to me. Teasing me?

For some reason this thought causes a little quiver along my nerves, not unlike a very mild version of the zaps his touch caused earlier.

'I felt as if I hadn't eaten for days.' I'm not going anywhere near that quiver, except to excuse it as tiredness. 'You can't count the plastic pack of two biscuits they gave me on the plane and a couple of minute chocolate bars I happened to find in my handbag. And speaking of food and planes, what do we do about eating on these trips to far-off places? Do we bring along a sandwich?'

Yeah, like that's possible. I've got cardamom pods, chocolate, and I'm pretty sure there's a half-full packet of teabags in my kitchen box, but not the one essential ingredient for even the simplest of sandwiches—bread.

'Of course you don't bring along a sandwich. We're working at hospitals wherever we go and we're always adequately fed.'

The words sound OK—I mean, he's explaining the set-up quite coherently—but he's frowning again, and the look on his face, kind of intent, makes me feel there's a hidden meaning lurking beneath the words. Though what kind of hidden meaning anyone can get out of hospital food is beyond me.

It has to be tiredness causing these weird thoughts. Tiredness and the zap-and-quiver routine.

I can't help thinking of my mother. Is this how she felt when she met the Argentinian polo player?

Was it electricity in his touch that led to my conception?

I haven't thought about these things for years, protected by my relationship with Pete—insured by it, you might say, against any extreme sexual reactions.

'Your job description is the same whether you're on this team or at a hospital,' GR is saying as I set aside thoughts of the mother I never knew and concentrate on his words. 'Only instead of being at the same large hospital all the time, you'll be doing sessions at different smaller hospitals.'

'Like working different wards, or in different rooms in Outpatients,' I offer, to show I'm with him on this. 'I can handle that.'

He frowns again.

'It isn't the work that bothers me,' he says, taking off his glasses and rubbing one hand across his face—suddenly looking even more tired than I feel. 'It's the situation. I'm sorry, we had a sudden post-partum bleed here in town late last night. I ended up having to do an emergency hysterectomy, then the sales started early so I didn't get much sleep. But we should talk about this.'

He returns the glasses to his nose and pushes them into place with a long, thin forefinger.

'I don't know what gave you the impression I didn't like working with women registrars,' he says, startling me back into the conversation. Though I can't remember whether he actually confirmed this, I had plenty of evidence.

I smile sweetly, tuck my hand under my chin in a thinking gesture and do a slow, 'Hmm. Could it have been Michael's jaw dropping so low I was afraid he'd dislocated it when he realised Dr Green was a woman? Or perhaps Maureen's distraught cry of ''Oh, no, they've sent a woman''? Then there was Georgia, choking on her half-eaten doughnut when I went to get my schedules. Just a few clues, which I think you confirmed earlier.'

The quirk happens again at the corner of his mouth, but he obviously isn't amused enough by my cheek for a full-blown smile.

Pity, really. It was something, that smile.

'You said you'd had trouble with women registrars in the past, though that didn't bother me as much as your disapproval of women specialising in O and G.'

'It's the hours,' he says, as if that explains everything.

'All doctors work crappy hours,' I remind him.

'But not all specialists!' He says this with the smug confidence of a man trumping his opponent's ace. 'ENT blokes are rarely called out in the middle of the night, neither are dermatologists, even ophthalmologists don't get many midnight emergencies—'

'So?' I—rudely, I guess—interrupt his list of people who don't get called out at night. 'Is there a point to this dissertation?'

He looks startled, then frowns, but says, humbly enough, 'Sorry. I tend to get carried away. The point I was making is that there are plenty of specialties women can follow that won't cause disruption to their households.'

The feminist bit of me stiffens immediately.

'You mean disrupt as in disturb the male of the household if one of the kids happens to wake while the woman is away delivering someone else's baby?'

'No, that's not what I mean. I'm all in favour of joint child-rearing responsibilities, but you've done enough O and G by now to know that the majority of women with young babies experience a higher than normal degree of tiredness. So, even if her partner is happy to feed the baby when she's called out, a woman O and G specialist, especially if she's still breast-feeding her infant, might not be firing on all cylinders on the job.'

'Fortunately enough, I'm not pregnant so won't be producing an infant, and being tired on the job during the six months I'm here,' I tell him, unable to help myself.

He sighs, shakes his head, then adds, 'I know I've put

that badly, but while in principle I believe women make excellent O and G specialists, in practice it's a hard job for them to pursue, and as a result a lot of them drop out. And that's what really gets my goat. They've taken up a keenly contested spot in the specialty programme, then they give up practice to have a family, and we're short of O and G specialists again.'

I open my mouth to argue, but he lifts a hand to cut me off.

'And don't tell me we're not short of them, because we are.'

I know that, but have always assumed it was because specialties like neurosurgery or heart transplants are more glamorous. I mean, you tell someone what you do, and the usual reaction is a grimace and that 'eugh' noise that people make when they pick up dog do on their shoe.

However, we're not talking other people here. We're talking GR Prentice and it's my turn to say something.

'And it's because you don't approve of women doing O and G you don't like women registrars?'

He sighs, studying me across the table as if I'm some new life form.

'You're like one of those sticky flies that buzz and buzz so persistently no amount of hand-waving ever chases them away.'

I have to smile at the description, because I know those flies. They choose you as their new best friend and *won't* go away. But understanding about flies is one thing, letting him off the hook without explaining is another.

'Hey, you're the one who suggested dinner so we could discuss this.'

He nods.

'Let's just say I've had bad luck with the three women

registrars I've had and leave it at that,' he says, but, of course, by now I really want to know.

'I'm one of those flies, remember. Did they wear ridiculous footwear? Was that the sin?'

He sighs again.

'Damn fly,' he mutters, but there's no rancour in it. 'The problem is that some people see a six-month posting to a place as remote as Bilbarra as an escape.'

He pauses, no doubt so I can take it in, but I'm not with him.

'From?' I prompt.

He waves one hand in the air.

'Whatever unpleasantness that is happening in their lives.'

'Do you know this for sure, or are you guessing?' I demand. 'I mean, Bilbarra is hardly the place any normal female would consider a safe haven from trouble. Most people haven't even heard of the place, and I would imagine, like me, the registrars you get are not given any choice in the matter. They're just sent, whether they want to go or not.'

'So you've not just broken up with your boyfriend? Not escaping to the country to get over your heartache?'

There's a funny little smile playing about his lips— different to the quirk—and it throws me. Does he know about Pete?

If I deny it, will he know I'm lying? Then suspect a lie in every word I say?

'As it happens, I did, not long ago, break up with my boyfriend but, believe me, if I wanted to escape, I'd have gone bigger, not smaller—headed to Sydney, or New York perhaps, definitely not Bilbarra. Which is why I'm saying maybe you made the wrong assumption about your other registrars. Surely, they, too, were sent here.'

'But you *are* nursing a broken heart?' he persists, and I groan.

'You called me a fly—what about this conversation? For your information, I am *not* nursing a broken heart. Yes, Pete and I had a relationship I thought would lead to marriage and it didn't, but that's not the end of the world.'

'No? You don't look very happy.'

I plaster a huge, false smile across my face.

'Well, I am, see! I'm happy!'

'Then why are you frowning?'

'You can't smile and frown at the same time, can you?' Boy, am I easily diverted! 'I didn't think facial muscles would work that way.'

'Well, you can,' he says, 'which means you can't be entirely overjoyed by this break-up you're trying to dismiss.'

It's my turn to sigh.

'I'm more puzzled than unhappy,' I admit, pleased, in an odd way, to have someone to explain it to. 'I mean, Pete and I are both intelligent, rational people. We met early in our years at med school and just sort of clicked. We had a relationship based on mutual interests and respect and deep affection then suddenly he meets a woman and whoom bang, bells sound, whistles blow, lights flash and he's fancying himself in love. I know it sounds more like a jackpot going off on a poker machine, but that's exactly how he explained it. As if!' I finish, shaking my head because the concept still seems totally bizarre to me.

'You don't believe in love?'

The question startles me.

'Of course I believe in love—as in a deep caring for someone. It's all around us in our relationships with family, as well as marriage. But this bells and whistles and flashing light stuff? No, I can't say I believe in that.'

Or electrical impulses zapping through fingers—I don't believe in them either, but I don't tell him this.

'So this man's defection meant nothing to you?'

'Of course it did, but it also provided me with a new beginning. You were right about O and G being a specialty that's hard to pursue when you're married with young children, but now that's off the agenda I can concentrate on my career.'

'Hmmm,' he says, so disbelieving I have to restrain myself from hurling my glass of water in his face.

What with the physical problems he causes, and dragging up the business with Pete, I'm a little twitchy.

Maybe a conversation change. He never did explain about women registrars—just diverted me into talking about Pete.

Deliberately?

We'll see.

'Anyway,' I say brightly, 'this isn't getting me any closer to understanding your antipathy to women registrars. I'll admit that maybe some of them *might* have come out here to escape something happening in their other lives, but is that so bad?'

He grins, says 'Fly' softly under his breath, then explains, in a long-suffering voice clearly intended to convey he's doing it under sufferance.

'My first woman registrar—back when this service started—had just broken up with her boyfriend or partner or whatever he was. Anyway, she gets out here, discovers she's pregnant, and not only pregnant but sick as a dog with it, and within three weeks the ex-boyfriend arrives and, whoosh, she's off back to the city.'

'Poor thing!' I mutter, though I don't put any heart into

it, certain the woman should have organised her life a little better.

One shapely eyebrow lifts at my expression of sympathy.

'Is that underwhelming compassion for being pregnant, being sick or getting back with the boyfriend?' he asks, and I have to laugh.

'All three, I guess, but you can't blame her for leaving under those circumstances.'

He lifts his shoulders in a casual shrug. They're good shoulders, not footballer broad but wide enough.

'No, I can't, but the next one who came was more trouble. She'd actually applied for my job, though I didn't know that, and had been knocked back because she lacked experience, and she thought...'

He stops and looks almost embarrassed, but as men rarely get embarrassed I decide I've misread his expression—I told you he wasn't easy to read.

I realise he hasn't paused but has actually stopped talking.

'You can't stop there,' I tell him. 'What did she think?'

He almost seems to be going pink and I contemplate the novel possibility of a man who blushes while he scowls at me, then stumbles into a flurry of words.

'If you must know, she thought she might marry me, and I know that sounds presumptuous, but it was hardly my fault. It made working with her very difficult and it was the worst six months of my life.'

He's so obviously embarrassed I decide to cut him some slack so, while my mind is whirling with the idea of a nice-looking man with twinkly grey eyes being abashed by a woman's interest in him, I steer him away from her.

'And the third? I think you said three.'

The third must have been special, for he smiles the kind of nostalgic smile people use for nice memories.

'The third was great, but unfortunately she was a bit like your ex. She met a man on the flight out to Bilbarra and, according to her, it was love at first sight. She stayed six months and was good at her job, but if I'd had to listen to one more minute of her praise of her wonder-man, or hear one more word about the magical romance they were enjoying long-distance—he's on a big cattle property north of here—I'd have strangled her.'

He pauses, then adds, 'And she left here to get married, and now she's on the property, which goes to prove what I was saying earlier, about losing women specialists from the service.'

He ends triumphantly, but I can't let him assume he's proved his point.

'I don't know why you're assuming she won't continue her career some time in the future. Surely having an extra O and G specialist out here in the outback is a good thing. This woman could provide back-up for the local GPs in her particular area. Isn't that why the second FOG service was set up? For better services out here in the bush?'

'It might be a good thing if she was working,' he said gloomily. 'But she's probably having babies of her own by now.'

'And that's bad? Populating the outback?'

He scowls at me.

'You're deliberately misunderstanding me,' he growls, the deep, slow voice even deeper. 'I don't know why I bothered trying to explain.'

'Especially when you're tired,' I offer helpfully, but he doesn't appreciate my understanding and scowls again.

'Let's drop the tired,' he says, and suddenly I'm feeling guilty.

Guilty about arguing with him—guilty about keeping him out of bed—heavens, I could go on for ever. Has anyone ever done a study on why women are more burdened with guilt than men?

But even while I'm grappling with guilt—and fighting the urge to apologise when none of what's happened or is happening is in any way my fault—I stand up to show I have no intention of keeping him up another minute.

In fact, I rather hope to convey the message that I'd have liked to have departed ages earlier. Not an easy message to convey without speech at the best of times, and virtually impossible in the confines of a busy Chinese restaurant where every second patron is calling a greeting to the man I'm trying to snub.

GR finally makes it to the desk, pays the bill and puts his hand in the small of my back to usher me out the door.

Now, Pete did this often enough, and I'm reasonably sure other men have made similar, polite hand-to-small-of-back contact but I've never previously responded as if jabbed by a cattle prod. I take an involuntary leap forward, miss the step that leads down to the exit, fall and bang my head—hard—against a case of no-doubt precious Chinese artefacts.

Cool hands fondle first one of my feet, then the other, and I sigh at the bliss of it, though vaguely aware it's my head that's hurting, not my feet.

'Come on, up you get.'

A strong arm circles my back and eases me first to a sitting position then, with further urging, back to my feet. By this time, half the diners have left their tables to have a look and my head clears sufficiently to realise I've made an idiot of myself on my first day in town. So much for medicos being held in respect by the general population!

Mortified, I want to get out of the place as quickly as possible, but GR insists on asking questions, touching me—which, incidentally, causes far more damage than the fall—and generally assuring himself—in a medical way—that nothing's broken.

'I'm OK. I never fall over. I must have slipped on something.' I'm lying through my teeth about the slipping but he's not to know that. 'Let's go.'

The proprietor has joined us, a Chinese woman looking so anxious she might burst into tears any moment. Is she worried I'll sue her?

I try to tell her it's OK, babbling on about it being my fault, though I've just denied this to GR. He tries to hush me, telling me everything's OK, then I realise she's not looking at me but at her cabinet which now has a long diagonal crack across the glass.

'And I'll get that fixed—or you get it fixed and send me the bill. The old nurses' quarters at the hospital. That'll find me. Will that find me?'

I turn to GR who's frowning quite ferociously.

'Stop worrying about the cabinet,' he says. 'Mrs Li knows it was an accident.' He's still steadying me with his arm around my back, and I realise the only way I'll escape his touch is to get out to the car. Ignoring the effects of it as much as possible I walk, carefully this time, out the door. It's only when a stone on the footpath bites into my sole that I realise I'm shoeless. My favourite silver sandals are dangling from the fingers of GR's left hand.

'I'll have my shoes back now, thanks.'

'You're probably safer barefoot,' he growls, then mutters something that sounds very like, 'As if!'

I make it to the car, wait patiently for him to unlock it and open the precious, buckle-prone aluminium door, then climb in. He hands me my shoes and our fingers tangle in the straps. He bends his head to sort things out, and I see his face in profile. It's just a face—a profile—yet something catches at my heart, and again I think of Pete.

And Claudia.

And my mother and the Argentinian.

And Mrs GR Prentice for surely there would be one…

Though there couldn't have been when the other registrar chased him…

I wake at four-thirty—bet you thought I'd sleep in! Not that waking early does me much good. I fell into bed last night too physically and emotionally exhausted by the experiences of the day to bother unpacking, so now I have to find where I packed some 'going to work' clothes.

They should, of course, be on the top of the second suitcase, because I put that much forethought into my packing, but one trip in the Cessna has reminded me that skirts of any kind are impossible—tight ones crawl up the thighs and full ones blow skyward in the wind that is generated especially for all airports.

I need pants—preferably cargo because they're loose enough to be comfortable in all day—and I know I've got a pair.

Somewhere!

By the time Michael arrives to collect me—well, I assumed when I heard the footsteps coming down the veranda that it was Michael, but the vibrations in the air make me turn and it isn't—I've got clothes strewn around the bit of the veranda that might, by some wild stretch of the imagination, be called the living area. I'm clad in an unexceptional T-shirt—white with a plasticky kind of bird printed on it—and a pair of bikini briefs that aren't as brief as beach-type bikinis but still probably not correct attire for greeting one's boss on the first morning of work.

'Two minutes!' I tell him, hoping he'll take the hint and depart, but he looks around with the air of a man visiting a museum of modern art. You know, one of those places where you're not sure if the paintings have been hung the right way up.

'Did you stay up all night to make this much mess?' he asks, but I've found a pair of jeans, and I'm scrabbling into them, hoping the open lid of the suitcase is providing me with some maidenly modesty.

'Aren't you early?' I demand, desperately sucking in my stomach in an attempt to get the zip done up. How long since I wore these jeans? Were they always tight or have the panic-easing chocolates I consumed since I heard about Bilbarra gone straight to my hips?

'I realised you hadn't had time to shop. Thought I'd take you for breakfast first. There's a transport café out along the road to the airport where Michael and I usually grab a snack and a coffee.'

Once the zip slid home, the button was easy. Maybe eating nothing but chocolate was a revolutionary kind of diet. I could write a book, make a fortune, retire from medicine—and leave Bilbarra.

Realising this isn't going to happen in time for me to get out of going to work today, I slide my feet into sandals—red and not quite as high in the heel as the silver disaster-causing ones from last night—grab the white coat and stethoscope I discovered early in the unpacking frenzy and prepare to follow GR out to his car.

'That's it?'

He's looking at me in a most peculiar manner.

I check I've got my jeans on even though I distinctly remember the struggle with the zip.

'I'm assuming they'll have pens and paper and pre-scription pads and whatever else I'll need at the hospital,' I tell him, puzzled by his reaction, but even more dis-turbed by the fact a good night's sleep hasn't changed the effect his presence has on my body.

'But no handbag? No receptacle full of the parapher-nalia women consider essential to daily life, so have to cart around with them?'

'You are the most judgmental man I've ever met,' I tell him, mentally banging my head against a wall. 'While as for generalisations…!'

I let him fill in the blanks and stride ahead of him. Of course I should have grabbed my handbag. There's floss in it, and nail clippers and a blister pack of paracetemol, which I'll probably need because this man's sure to give me a headache before the day is over. And some mois-turiser, essential in the dry air out here—although most hospitals have great moisturiser the physio uses for mas-sage and the nurses use on patients to prevent their skin drying out in the air-conditioning—and nearly a whole block of fruit and nut chocolate if I remember rightly…

And my wallet and credit card! I'm wailing silently to myself by now. I hate going *anywhere* without my credit card. I'm not a shopaholic—mainly because of chocolate, as I believe being two kinds of '-aholic' would be overkill and definitely show addictive tendencies. And I've already explained my inherent miserliness in things like paying unnecessary rent, but I have to admit I've small spending weaknesses in other areas.

But there's no way I'm going back for my handbag and, what's worse, I'm now stuck with six months of not carrying a bag, if only to prove this man wrong. I'll have to tuck things into my pockets. I definitely need to find the cargo pants—cargo pants have great pockets—and probably buy a few more pairs.

I must have groaned because GR catches up with me.

'What was that?' he asks, opening the car door and peering over it at me. His chin is freshly shaven so his skin has a shiny look, and I really, really want to run my hand across it to see if it feels as smooth as it looks.

Handbags, or lack of same, I realise as I climb aboard, are really very minor irritations compared to the major stuff going on inside me.

I ignore his question and he doesn't repeat it, settling into the driver's seat, buckling up, speaking quietly as he goes efficiently about the business of getting us on the way.

'Blythe and Callum Whitworth are the doctors at Creamunna—husband and wife medical team, not long married. Both good, caring doctors.'

Once again small talk consists of the imparting of information GR feels I should have. I resist the urge to ask whether she'll be less good and caring when she's breast-feeding her first infant. Five-thirty in the morning isn't the ideal time to be starting an argument.

'They've both done obstetric short courses and are happy to take uncomplicated pregnancies through to term.'

He's pulling up at a dusty-looking roadhouse as he speaks, but the remark is puzzling enough for me to query it.

'You say that as if it's unusual. I know GPs in the city refer pregnant patients on to specialists, but I thought, out here, they would all do some obstetric work.'

'They do to a certain extent, but in a lot of country areas the women then go to the nearest city to give birth. I'm at Bilbarra, and there's an O and G specialist in

Mount Isa, but generally speaking women go across to the larger hospitals on the coast a few weeks before they're due.'

'But that's terrible. What about their friends and family? How can they share the excitement if the newborn is hundreds of kilometres away?'

The little quirk of a smile appears and disappears so quickly I wonder if I've imagined it, but I've remembered his conversation at the restaurant.

'Surely that's an argument for more women coming out to you as registrars. You marry them off to locals and, *voilà*, once they've had their own families, you've got O and G services in the bush!'

Definitely no smile this time. I get the frown again.

'You're deliberately misunderstanding the situation,' he grumbles, hauling his long, lean body out of the car and striding around to open the door on my side.

I beat him to it, not because of feminist issues but because I don't want him standing too close to me again. Mental note—buy cargo pants in size larger than normal, I'm going to need a lot of chocolate to get through the next six months.

I'm also going to have to rethink the heeled sandals, I realise as I try not to stumble in and out of the potholes littering the ground between me and breakfast. I know I swore—back when I left home—that I'd never wear elastic-sided boots again, but out here they're sensible footwear.

Essential shopping list now reads cargo pants and boots—and the chocolate I brought with me won't be nearly enough so add that as well. And I really should get some bread and butter and a few tins of baked beans—beans on toast being my staple diet when left to feed myself.

GR has not only caught up with me by now, but overtakes me. Mercifully, he refrains from commenting on my unhappy progress.

Until we're seated at the table, breakfast ordered—bacon, eggs, sausages and tomatoes for him, a slice of raisin toast and cup of coffee for me. The single slice is only because I realise I need to keep a few hundred calories up my sleeve for some recovery chocolate when I get back to the quarters.

'Didn't you give any thought to a suitable wardrobe when you were told you were coming out here?' he asks.

It's one of those times I wish I could raise one eyebrow. Raising both just doesn't have the same effect.

'I tried not to think about it at all,' I tell him, which is true. Some things I think about too much and end up so confused I wish I hadn't started. So I'm retraining myself. It's a coping mechanism. Don't think about it and it might go away.

It never does, of course. Not thinking about Pete meeting Claudia didn't make her go away. Though Pete did…

'Good grief! What's wrong now? I only asked a question. It's not as if I berated you.'

The words don't make sense until I realise he's leaned across the table and is using a pristine white handkerchief to mop at my cheeks.

I'm crying?

But I never cry!

Well, maybe a little when Grandad died.

And when I see newborn babies.

And sometimes when a sunset is particularly beautiful….

And when—

I sniff and shake my head, not wanting his hand so close to my face.

'I'm not really crying,' I tell him. 'It's just my eyes leak sometimes.'

Where this has come from I've no idea, but once it pops out, it doesn't seem too bad an excuse.

'Oh, I see,' he says, tucking the handkerchief into my hand—no doubt because of the sniff, and I do need it, that's something else that was in my handbag—then leaning back in his chair. 'Leaking eyes? You've seen someone about them?'

I blow my nose—hard—on his handkerchief, then realise I can't give it back. Try to ram it into my pocket, but the panic-chocolates have made the pocket almost non-existent. I slide my hand inside the neck of the T-shirt and tuck it down my bra instead, thinking I can transfer it to the pocket of my white coat when I get back to the car, but throughout this process I can feel GR's eyes on me—watchful, puzzled, wary.

Fortunately Michael arrives, dead-heating with our breakfast. He orders coffee and a toasted sandwich to go, though, after seeing him on the plane yesterday, I wonder about his choice.

'I don't eat it,' he whispers when GR gets up to speak to someone at the back of the restaurant, 'but the boss seems to think we should all eat something before we leave, so I order it to keep him happy.'

'If ordering a toasted sandwich to go guarantees keeping him happy, maybe I should order a couple of dozen,' I say, and Michael laughs, though I can see he's wound as tightly as a spring.

'Why are you doing this job when you suffer motion sickness?' I ask, but GR's back at the table and Michael doesn't answer.

Does he think the man he calls 'the boss' doesn't know he almost pukes every time he gets in a moving vehicle?

CHAPTER FOUR

WE HEAD out to the airport in separate vehicles, and join Dave at the plane—well, I think it's Dave until GR does this 'Bob, Blue, Blue, Bob' routine again.

'I'm Dave's twin,' Bob says as he shakes my hand, grinning at what must be my obvious confusion.

'Are you OK with being called the wrong name?' I ask, knowing I'll never get them straight.

'We're both used to it,' Bob assures me, and reaches out to help me climb in.

GR makes a hmphing noise behind me, but I'm getting used to his unspoken comments now and ignore it. Though ignoring him is harder, especially when he turns towards me as we taxi, no doubt to check I'm buckled in. I wait for him to say something, but all he does is look at me then frown, as if he can't remember who I am or why I'm in the plane with him.

Creamunna from the air looks fresh and green so they must have a good water supply. The man who collects us from the airport talks cattle to GR, so I have time to look around. There's a wide brown river—the source of the water?—flowing sluggishly beside the road on the out-skirts of the town, with fat-trunked gums throwing dark shadows on the water.

'There'd be lobbies in that river,' I tell Michael, think-ing of the little freshwater crayfish I caught in dams as a child. 'Boiled up with lots of salt and an onion, they're delicious.'

Michael shudders as if shellfish are as nauseating as

flying, then I realise it's the mention of food that's upset him.

'Do you take something to help it?' I ask him, and he shrugs then lifts his shirt. He's got a brown paper bag strapped to his stomach.

'Mrs Jenks, my landlady, suggested this. It hasn't worked any better than ginger tablets, heavy drugs or wearing garlic on my person.'

'You'd have thought the garlic would have worked,' I tell him, as we turn into a circular drive in front of the hospital. 'If only because whoever was flying would have put you out of the plane.'

He manages a weak grin, and we both disembark. I'm anxious to see the hospital and no doubt, now the flight's over, he's anxious to eat something. I hope it isn't the greasy toasted sandwich.

A tall, well-built woman with wavy blonde hair comes out of the building, and greets GR with a kiss and a hug.

'And how are you?' he asks, easing her back to arm's length and examining a body that's thickening with pregnancy.

'So well Cal says it's obscene,' she says, glowing good-naturedly at GR.

'It's beautiful,' GR says quietly, but I hear the words, and I must admit I'm surprised. Not a man to be showering compliments around at will, I wouldn't have thought.

'I've come to ask you all to lunch,' she continues, though there's a pinkness in her cheeks from his compliment. 'It will be salads and cold meat so any time that suits you. I know you've got Grandchester this afternoon, but you have to eat.'

GR accepts for all of us, introduces me, though this time uses my name.

'Hillary's an unusual name,' Blythe says, smiling warmly as she shakes my hand. Then she pats her tummy. 'As you might guess, I'm name-conscious at the moment.' She turns back to Gregor. 'I like Gregor, too—it's a good strong name for a boy—but Cal growls every time I mention it.'

She winks at GR. 'Which perhaps I do a little oftener than necessary.'

I get a warm feeling that, this time, has nothing to do with the presence of the boss. It's because this woman oozes such blissful contentment, it permeates the air like a glorious perfume.

I blink, but it's the dry air—nothing more—that makes me think my eyes might leak again.

Then we're on the move once more, Blythe heading out towards the car park while we enter the hospital. A nurse in a soft aqua uniform greets GR and Michael, more introductions, then she, Pam, waves the men away and leads me down a corridor.

'This is the consulting room. The trolley's set up for you, but if there's anything else you need, give a shout. That's the patient list and files,' she adds, pointing to a list on the desk and a tray of files beside it.

She smiles, then adds, 'If I'd known we were finally getting another woman O and G registrar I'd have asked Blythe to make an appointment for me.'

'You've a problem?'

She shrugs as if it's not important, hesitates, then finally says, 'It's probably nothing, but just lately I've been finding intercourse very painful. I've tried using creams—actually, I got my sister to send me some because no way was I walking into the chemist here in town to buy something like that.'

'How old are you?' I ask.

'Thirty-eight. I thought of early menopause, but Blythe did a blood test and my oestrogen levels are fine.'

'How busy am I this morning?' I ask her, and she shakes her head.

'You're full up, but I'll make an appointment to see you next month.'

Somewhere in my head there's some information that suggests this isn't the answer, but I can't retrieve it right now, and Pam's already heading for the door to rustle up my first patient.

Jane Evans has been having heavy, painful periods since her first child was born, and I suspect fibroids. I can feel a mass when I palpate her abdomen, but she'll need a laparoscopy to really tell.

'We make a small incision in your abdomen and insert a little tube that carries a fibre-optic instrument that allows us to see what's in there on a screen. If they're small enough,' I explain, 'we can insert a laser through the same tube and remove them.'

'And if they're not small enough?'

'You might require more extensive surgery.' I'm hesitant and know she senses it, but she's young, and probably wants more children, so I don't want to mention the possibility of a hysterectomy.

She thinks about this for a moment, then decides she wants to know more. I love it when women make this decision for themselves, rather than having it foisted on them with a doctor giving too much information all at once. I'm guilty of having done that, I know, but I *try* not to repeat my mistakes.

'We're not sure why fibroids form,' I explain, 'but suspect it's the result of some damage to the wall of the uterus during pregnancy that doesn't heal properly, so a small, hard lump forms. These lumps are benign, but they cause problems like the ones you're having.'

'If they're small enough,' Jane says, repeating what I've said earlier. 'And if they're not?'

'If we can't get them through a laparoscope, then we could do a laparotomy, which means we make a bigger cut in your abdomen, as we would for a Caesarean operation, and get at them that way.'

'So I can still have children afterwards?'

This is crunch time again.

'Yes. Even without removing them you could have more children. The only problem is if they are very bad and cause you a great deal of pain. Then I might sometimes recommend a hysterectomy, and you'd have to think about whether that's what you want.'

'Well, at least I've got Will,' Jane says, 'and I was an only child and I don't think I suffered because of it.'

I want to hug her, she's so brave and forthright. I'd probably have howled like a baby if someone had told me that.

We discuss the laparoscopy some more and I tell her I'll book her for it next month.

'Will you do it?' she asks.

'I think so,' I tell her, and realise why I won't be able to see Pam on our next visit. GR will be doing the consulting!

I'm still thinking about this—the division of labour—when I finish with the patients. I'm running late, there's lunch, then a plane trip to the next town for afternoon consultations.

'I know it's hard but you have to try to keep to the timetable,' GR tells me as we head for the hospital car. The same guy who picked us up is waiting by it. I wonder what happens to our pilot while we're in town. Does someone take him out a cuppa? Does he bring a packed lunch and Thermos?

'Because of the flights and the restrictions on the pilot's flying hours we can't get too far behind.'

GR's still talking while I'm worrying over the pilot's morning tea. Then I remember what I was worrying about when I finished the morning's work.

'You said you used to go turn and turn about, operating and consulting, when you had a male registrar, but while you're stuck with me, in case someone would prefer to see a woman, do you think we should do half and half so we both do some consulting each visit?'

'No.'

He doesn't say it rudely, just in such an uncompromising manner it should have ended the argument immediately.

Unfortunately, uncompromising manners tend to rile me.

'No? Just like that? No discussion? No, is there some reason you're asking? You just say no and that finishes things?'

'Usually,' he says, and sighs so loudly it's a wonder he doesn't blow the paint off the car.

Michael is smiling, though discreetly, and I'm sorry I wasted my sympathy on him earlier.

Then I think of Pam, having to wait two months before I'm consulting again. Two months of painful intercourse.

'Well, now I understand that, would you make my excuses to Blythe? There's someone else I need to see here. I'm sure the hospital will rustle up a sandwich for me.'

GR looks shell-shocked, as if no one ever argues with his plans.

'And how will you get back to the airport?'

'I'd have thought you could have the driver swing past

here and pick me up. I'll only be half an hour—it will take you that long to eat lunch.'

He's about to argue—I can see it in the way he's looking at me, so I rush into speech again.

'Look, I understand about schedules, and keeping to them, and eating proper meals, and I guarantee I'll get better at it, but this is Pam, the nurse who was working with me. She's probably known you since you started the service from Bilbarra and feels embarrassed talking about something personal with you. I don't want her to have to wait another two months to see me, which is what she'll do if I don't see her now.'

GR nods, but it's one of those sharp, accepting kind of nods, not a kindly, understanding one.

So who cares? That's what I ask myself as I hurry back to the hospital to catch Pam before she dashes off to some new duty.

'No, I was writing up the schedules for next month's visit,' she tells me when I find her still at the desk outside the consulting room. 'Then going to lunch.'

'How about I examine you first?' I suggest, and she looks surprised.

'Oh, no, that wouldn't be right. I can wait until next month,' she says. 'I know Blythe asked you all to lunch because there was a new registrar coming in. That's you.'

'I can talk to Blythe some other time, but I won't be consulting next month, I'll be operating,' I explain, and Pam finally gives in.

'I thought it might have been endometriosis,' she explains as she strips off and climbs on the examination table. 'But I don't have any other symptoms, and last time I was in Brisbane I arranged to have a laparoscopy to check and there was no sign of it.'

She sighs then adds, 'But knowing it wasn't endo didn't make the discomfort any better.'

A physical examination doesn't reveal anything that could be causing the problem, so we talk sex for a while—whether she enjoys it, how much foreplay she and her husband indulge in, whether she enjoys regular orgasms.

See why she didn't want to talk to GR! This is the kind of thing we have to talk about in cases of dyspareunia, which is the fancy name for painful intercourse.

'Has Blythe run any thyroid tests?' I ask after we've ruled out arthritic problems in the hips or lower back. 'An underactive thyroid could cause a drying up of the secretions. In the meantime, I'll write you a script for an oestrogen cream, which is better than over-the-counter creams, and I could easily be prescribing it for menopausal symptoms so you shouldn't feel embarrassed getting it filled at the chemist. Use the cream sparingly—every second or third day—over the next month. I'll let Blythe know and suggest the thyroid test and I'll talk to you next month.'

I'm scribbling away—first the script, then the note to Blythe, as Pam's GP.

'I'll get Blythe to do a referral, too, so the paperwork is in order,' Pam says, then she adds, 'Thanks.'

I'm waiting dutifully under a tree near the front drive when the car pulls up. We drive back to the airport in silence, which suits me, though inside I'm thinking of so many things my mind's getting fogged up. Although this worked out for Pam, I'm not going to be able to see every woman who'd prefer not to see a man, any more than GR's going to see all the patients who want to talk to a man.

I don't mention these niggling concerns, assuming GR in particular would treat them with disdain. We had a lecturer at uni who was always telling us we couldn't cure everyone.

'You know we can't possibly see every patient in western Queensland.' GR confirms my unspoken thoughts as he waits for me to get in the plane.

'No, but we can try,' I snap, answering the lecturer from long ago as much as GR.

He looks startled, then smiles, and the smile starts heat driving downwards through my body and sending a cloud of redness into my brain so all rational thought ceases.

Gregor.

Although well aware of the dangers of even mentally acknowledging the effect he has on me, I try his name silently to myself. Blythe said it was a strong name and she was right, but it's also unusual enough to help the bearer of it distance himself—if he happens to be that kind of man, which, in my limited experience of him, GR certainly is.

Though I have to stop the GR stuff I'm doing in my head, or I'll inadvertently call him that to his face one day.

It's at this stage I realise I'm maybe obsessing over him, and try to write a mental shopping list instead. Though when I'll ever have time to shop, I have no idea.

The rest of the day is fairly predictable. No patient runs amok with a knife—that's a rarity among O and G patients anyway, and more likely to happen in city hospital emergency departments than out here—the plane doesn't crash, I don't hurl myself in GR's arms, though from time to time I wonder just how it would feel to have him hold me.

I'm lying about the 'from time to time'. Practically all the time we're together—in the car, in the plane—I think about it. I know it's just an inexplicable physical attraction which, of course, I'll resist. But I'm also just a teensy weensy bit jealous of those women I keep reading about in books who positively leap from one affair to another, not for an instant considering resistance, and relishing the opportunity to enjoy guilt-free physical satisfaction.

The problem is, those women weren't brought up by my grandmother, who, while not big on guilt—never once did she criticise what happened when my mother gave in to physical attraction—somehow instilled in me a sense of personal responsibility. And then for so long there was Pete, so fooling around every time my hormones got a buzz from an attractive man wasn't an option.

I try to remember an attractive man giving me a buzz— pre-GR, that is. These thoughts occupy the entire trip back from Grandchester to Bilbarra. Not exactly enlivening when I realise how few attractive men there've been in my life. In fact, if you want to know how many have cast themselves across my path in an agony of unrequited love, then it's nil. I think that happens more to blondes and maybe tall, languid brunettes. Short redheads barely count in the greater scheme of lovelorn swains.

'Did you leave lights on in the quarters this morning?'

I'm back in GR's car—I think it's kindness on his part that he's chauffeuring me around. Kindness to Michael, not me. He must know how nauseous Michael gets and realises the poor guy wouldn't want me watching him throw up.

We've pulled up outside the nurses' quarters, and light is shining brightly through the louvres.

'I don't think so, but I could have done,' I tell him, opening the car door and sliding out—anxious to get away from him.

'I'll walk in with you,' he announces, and ushers me

towards the steps, and although his hand isn't touching the small of my back, I swear I can feel the heat of it there.

I open the door, and wonder if I'm in the right place. My suitcases, and the hastily flung-about clothing, have disappeared, there's a glass bottle with an arrangement of feathery grass on the television, and a scrumptious aroma of food is drawing my feet down the veranda.

Gran appears before we've gone two paces.

'Oh, there you are. A nice woman at the hospital told me you usually got back about now. And you've brought a friend. It's a good thing I made plenty of hotpot.'

'Hotpot!' I swallow the saliva that's flooding my mouth. Gran's hotpot is legendary. People have been known to detour five hundred kilometres out of their way for a plate of it.

I hug Gran and my eyes leak just a little bit because it's ages since I've seen her, then I introduce her to GR.

'He's not a friend, he's my boss,' I explain, realising, as I say it, it's impolite, but it's the truth, isn't it? 'He's just dropping me back from the airport.'

That's to let both of them know he's not staying.

'And I suppose you have to get home to your wife and family,' Gran says, and though I've kept telling myself the man must surely be married, I hold my breath while I wait for his reply.

'No wife, no family, Mrs Green,' he says easily, then he sniffs the air so blatantly I want to kick him. 'And whatever that is certainly smells great.'

Gran beams at him. Feeding people is her favourite thing. I want to explain this to GR. That it doesn't mean anything, that Gran isn't trying to throw us together. But if he's not thinking that, then I'd make a fool of myself mentioning it so I keep quiet.

'Go and wash your hands, Hillary,' she says, and suddenly I'm eight again. I go, but only to hide the heat that's flared into my cheeks. I wash my hands, then come out to find GR standing by the kitchen sink.

'I've done mine,' he says, holding them out for inspection, and I look, not at them but up into his face. The quirky smile is there, and I have to smile back, although my heart is racing and my knees are shaking.

I realise I could probably cope with purely physical attraction, but if he's going to prove to have a sense of humour as well…

'Come and eat,' Gran says, from over by the table. 'I couldn't find a tablecloth among your things, Hillary, so I borrowed one from the hospital. I'll speak to you later about slackness and general untidiness.'

GR's lips quirk again.

'That silly half-smile is losing its attraction,' I whisper viciously at him. 'It was your fault I left clothes lying everywhere—taking me out to dinner last night when I could have been unpacking and—'

'Making you fall over,' he puts in helpfully.

I ignore him and finish with, 'Coming early this morning. That's what I was going to say.'

'If I hadn't come early you wouldn't have had breakfast—if you can call a slice of toast breakfast.'

Gran's joined us at the table, pot in one hand, ladle in the other.

'I knew she wasn't eating properly,' she says. Trust Gran to join the enemy. Whatever happened to blood being thicker than water? 'As soon as she walked in. Mind you, there wasn't anything to eat in the place—apart from chocolate and some herbs and spices—until I shopped, and don't tell me you'd have eaten hospital food, young lady, because I know how much you hate it.'

She's ladling hotpot—meat, potatoes, onions, carrots and rich, sumptuous gravy—onto my plate as she nags, so the scowl I give her lacks venom. I change the subject.

'This is great, Gran,' I tell her. 'And it's wonderful to see you, but what's Bilbarra got that enticed you away from Rosebud?'

'Memories,' Gran says, but so quietly she's drowned out by GR's sudden interest in the conversation.

'Rosebud Station?' he asks Gran. 'Up Julia Creek way? I've bought breeding stock from there. Would Joel be your son? Joel Green—of course.' He looks at me and shakes his head. 'I didn't make the connection. Is Joel your father?'

'He's my uncle, and why should you make a connection?' I say, though part of my mind would rather have pursued Gran's answer. Memories? 'I'm a city Green while Joel's country through and through.'

Gran gives a snort of disbelief. She keeps telling me there's too much country in my blood for me to ever leave it completely.

Anyway, the conversation now shifts to cattle breeding. Apparently GR has a property not far out of Bilbarra, run by a manager, and although this area is not drought-prone, he's been looking at breeding more drought resistance into his stock. Hence the purchase of the Rosebud stock.

As the two chat on, I look more closely at Gran. Well, it's that or looking more closely at GR which, as you know, is dangerous. Maybe it's not having seen her for a while, but suddenly I see her as an attractive woman. Mature—she's never mentioned her age but she's got to be in her seventies—but still attractive with the same green eyes I inherited, but with slightly helped honey-blonde hair cut in a short, no-nonsense bob.

Grandad's been dead ten years now. Does she still miss him? Does she get lonely?

And suddenly I'm pleased to have her here, not so much in the old role of caregiver, or even as a relative, but as someone who could well become a friend.

'She was always like that,' Gran's saying, as I come out of my thoughts to find my companions staring at me. 'When she was a little girl and went off like that, she used to say she got lost in her head, and I suppose that's as good a way of describing it as any.'

'Well, thank you for sharing that embarrassment with the world,' I snap at her, forgetting all thoughts of friendship.

'I promise I won't repeat it,' GR says, positively beaming with delight at having something to hold over me. 'This meal is delicious, Mrs Green. I'm a great fan of one-pot meals. I bought myself a slow-cooker and often set it going before I leave for work in the morning, so I can come home to a decent meal.'

He's got to be joking! If I tried to visualise GR snipping carrots into a pot, I'd be lost in my head for ever. Call me a cynic but I'm sure he's making it up to curry favour with Gran. Next thing he'll be asking for a recipe.

Fortunately he doesn't, mainly because Gran's asking him why a man like him has to rely on a slow-cooker for a decent meal.

'You're good-looking enough, so why aren't you married?'

Subtlety was never Gran's strong point, so it isn't her question that's surprised me but GR's reaction. The light's not all that good so I couldn't swear to it, but I'm sure his cheeks, dark with what's now a nine o'clock shadow, have taken on a delicate pinkish hue. It happened once before and I thought I'd imagined it, but now…

A man his age, which must be thirty-plus, who blushes?

He finishes the last mouthful of food on his plate, then looks around as if seeking a diversion that will provide a satisfactory switch in the conversation. No little green men appear, no carpet snake winds down from the ceiling, there's no explosion over at the hospital, so he's forced to either be rude and ignore her, or to answer.

'It just hasn't happened, that's all,' he says, voice gruff, probably with anger at being forced into this situation. Then he smiles at Gran and relaxes back into his chair. 'I suppose the right woman hasn't come along.'

'And do you have an image of this "right" woman?' Gran asks, and I'm pretty sure she's not being facetious.

I would have been if it had been me asking the question.

GR hesitates then seems to realise that hesitation won't wash with Gran. Neither will changing the subject. She'll allow you a little respite, then home right back onto the subject like a heat-seeking missile.

'I guess everyone has a hazy image of their perfect match. Shared interests, much the same physical characteristics as yourself so physically you're well matched that way. Similar emotional balance.'

So he wants a tall, quiet, unemotional brunette whose eyes don't leak.

'I've never said that to anyone before,' he adds, as if the answer was a revelation to himself as well, and now he's said it the conversation is finished.

He doesn't know Gran!

'Earlier you said it just hadn't happened. What's never happened?'

Talk about pinning a man to a spot. If it wasn't for the zapping I'd have felt sorry for him.

GR shrugs, inevitably drawing my attention to his well-

constructed shoulders. The man might be lean, but there's
strength in that leanness, and hard, flat planes of muscle
that stretch his shirt whenever he moves.

'Meeting someone like that and—well, falling in love,
I guess,' he's saying to Gran when I've reminded myself
his muscles are none of my business and tune in again to
the conversation. 'I don't mean physical attraction—that
rash madness that makes grown men act like fools—but
the deep abiding love that grows and strengthens as two
people share their lives. I know love's a subject most men
avoid like the plague, and I'll admit, when I was young,
I was fairly cynical about the existence of an emotion that
couldn't be proven or quantified in any way. But I've seen
enough happy relationships to accept that something exists to make them work as well as they do. My parents
are a prime example. They're not what you'd call romantic, yet being together has worked for them for forty
years.'

Gran beams at him as if having happily married parents
is his doing, while I just stare at him in disbelief.

He's got to be making this up. GR Prentice, the man
who doesn't approve of women O and G specialists, who
hates having the hassle of woman registrars working for
him, is a closet romantic? I've only known the man a
couple of days, but my mind's definitely boggling.

'That proves it must be love you're waiting for,' Gran
tells him, throwing me a don't-you-dare look as if she
knows I'd like to make a vomit sound. 'Having grown up
with a wonderful example of a happy marriage in action,
you're not willing to settle for anything less.'

GR smiles, as if agreeing with her, then says, 'It's been
quite a wait.'

The words, quietly spoken, carry a trace of regret and
I forget my cynicism for long enough to wonder if he's

telling the truth. If he really is a man who's looking for love!

Gran nods understandingly.

'But you'll find it's worth it in the end. I waited until the real thing came along, and you know where I found it?' She's beaming at him as if he's about to win a million dollars if he guesses right, then doesn't give him a chance to answer. 'Right here in Bilbarra,' she announces, nodding to confirm the words. 'Literally right here.'

She waves her arms around then turns towards the windows above the sink and smiles nostalgically.

'I came out here for my first job as a fully fledged nursing sister, and Hillary's grandfather was managing a property not far out of town. In those days these quarters were connected up to the hospital, and if you came back after midnight—that's when our leave passes finished—the outside door was locked, and you had to walk in through the hospital. Of course, someone always reported you to Matron.'

She smiles again and nods towards the windows.

'Many's the night Jock boosted me up through those windows.'

'You climbed through the windows? Grandad boosted you up? What were you doing, running around Bilbarra until after midnight anyway?'

As soon as that last bit came out I realised what she'd probably been doing, and knew the colour in my cheeks was more a deep scarlet than a delicate pink. But, honestly, if there's one thing a woman doesn't need to know about, it's her grandparents' sex lives.

Fortunately GR is talking, asking Gran about the property Grandad managed, and, of course, as the fates are currently joined in a conspiracy against me, it's the place he now owns, and he's inviting Gran to visit this weekend.

That's enough to shock my mind away from the previous conversation.

'Come out and stay,' he adds expansively. 'Hillary's on call but it's only fifteen minutes from town and it takes longer than that to get the aircraft ready for take-off.'

'Gran can go,' I tell him. 'I've got things to do this weekend. If every day's as long as today, I won't have time during the week to shop or sort things out here.'

'I can do that for you.' Ever-helpful Gran. I want to ask how long she's staying—I can probably keep from strangling her for three weeks, but after that, if she keeps up this matchmaking business, because I know full well that's what it is, I won't be responsible for my actions. But asking her point blank would probably sound rude to GR so I restrain myself.

'Good, I'll tell Elizabeth, my manager's wife, to expect all three of us,' GR says, then he pushes back his chair, reaches out for my plate and Gran's, stacks all three then carries them across to the sink.

'I'll wash those later,' Gran tells him, bustling after him. 'Would you like a cup of tea or coffee?'

GR shakes his head.

'No, thank you. The meal was wonderful, but I've got to go. I've a patient to see at the hospital, and another early morning tomorrow.'

His eyes meet mine across the top of Gran's head.

'You've got the schedule? You know tomorrow's three towns—Gilgudgel, where we should be able to check on yesterday's new arrival, then Edenvale, then Amberton.'

He smiles down at Gran who's been given more smiles in a couple of hours than I've seen him use in two days. He'll wear his lips out at this rate!

'We get home at about the same time, but I won't stay on for a meal. It would be too easy to get into the habit of being fed, then, when you leave, I'd have to rely on Hillary.'

Gran rolls her eyes.

'From the amount of chocolate I unpacked out of her boxes, I'd say you're more likely to get half a bar of special dark than a decent meal.'

'Chocoholic?' He swivels towards me and the eyebrow rises.

'Chocolate has been proven to have a number of calmative properties,' I tell him snootily.

It's also good for despair, depression, worry, panic and when you don't have a date on a Saturday night. Of course, not having a date on a Saturday night requires heavy-duty chocolate consumption. Try blending chocolate milk, chocolate ice cream, chocolate sauce and your favourite chocolate bar with a dash of chocolate liqueur and sip while eating double chocolate fudge ice cream straight from the container.

'It's no good, she's gone again,' Gran says as she walks GR along the veranda to the front door.

He turns, and this time he smiles at me. Me, not Gran. I'm not hyperventilating, though I'm close. Panic chocolate is something small enough to eat in handfuls. Little chocolate beans or buds you can toss right down. Broken bits off bars are too chunky and could cause choking during panic times. Doctors know these things!

I wonder where Gran put the packets when she unpacked.

CHAPTER FIVE

KNOWING Gran's visit was prompted by an urge to revisit her happy memories of the past doesn't make accepting her presence any easier. It's a long time since we've lived together, but not long enough for her to have got out of the habit of being the carer, me the caree. Which, in Gran's mind, means I still have to be told what to do.

Like washing my hands before a meal and eating a proper breakfast. Believe me, I do both those things on a regular basis, but Gran feels duty-bound to remind me.

The argument is over breakfast.

'Michael and…' I stall, not wanting to call him GR to Gran and unable to say Gregor out loud '…the boss stop for breakfast at the roadhouse on the way to the airport so, whichever of them comes to give me a lift, I'll have a chance to get something there.'

'I stopped there for fuel on the way into town,' Gran informs me. 'The facilities weren't the cleanest. You tell those two from me that while I'm here I'll cook their breakfasts.'

'No, Gran. No way. I work with these guys but I don't need them in my life twenty-four seven.'

'Twenty-four seven? What on earth are you talking about?'

I have to smile.

'Not up with things, Gran?' I tease, because she prides herself in keeping up to date with what's going on in the world. 'It's part of the new conversational shorthand people use these days. Twenty-four hours a day, seven days a week. When it's written there's a slash between the two numbers.'

And having successfully diverted her from the subject of breakfast, I push a few necessities into the pockets of my cargo pants—which Gran found among the debris of clothes on the veranda and left, folded neatly, in a drawer in my room—and go out to meet GR who's just pulling up outside.

'Don't you dare come out and offer him breakfast,' I warn Gran, who looks offended then goes to the louvres to wave to him. Maybe it's because she taught me at home herself—Rosebud was a hundred kilometres from the nearest town—and never had the opportunity to wave me off to school, but she stands there and waves as we leave.

'Is she staying long, your grandmother?' GR asks, and I realise this is probably the first personal conversation we've had—apart from when he's commented on my clothing.

'Who knows?' I reply, then vent a little spleen. 'That's the problem with unexpected visitors. It's always nice to see people you like, but eventually you want to get your life back. But if you ask them how long they're staying it sounds rude.'

GR glances my way then turns his attention back to the road. I can't see the eyebrow but I'm pretty sure it's risen.

'You're unable to lead a normal life with your grandmother around? Does she cramp your style? Stop you throwing wild parties? Prevent you having men in your room night after night?'

'I've never found sarcasm either clever or amusing,' I tell him, and fortunately we're now at the roadhouse so conversation can cease. Considering Michael's dicky stomach, I don't really want to travel with him, and buying myself a car in order not to travel with GR seems like a bit of overkill.

Maybe a push-bike. I'd be getting exercise, which would be a double benefit, given the chocolate I'll undoubtedly need to keep me sane.

'Aren't you coming in?'

He's holding the door open, that familiar look of pained patience on his face.

I slide out—these big four-wheel-drives are too high off the ground to make getting in and out easy for short people and, with him holding the door, I land within the ambit of the voltage. I'm trying for a kind of casual elegance to combat this, but my left foot lands on a rock and I stumble, only slightly.

I can feel GR's impatience with my footwear vibrating in the air between us.

'Before you decided to whisk us off to your property for the weekend, I'd intended spending Saturday morning checking out the local shoe stores for a decent pair of boots,' I tell him haughtily. 'I'm not totally stupid.'

'Store,' he says, and I must look bewildered, for he adds helpfully, 'There's only one, and we don't have to leave early, so you can shop before we go. In fact, if you like, I'll collect you at nine and take you to it.'

A rather hazy memory of cool hands on my feet makes me shiver with apprehension.

'No—thanks but, no, it's OK. Gran has a car. I'll drive myself.'

Inside, Michael's sipping at a cup of weak tea.

'I've ordered your breakfast,' he says to GR, 'but didn't know what Hillary ate.'

'Hardly anything, apart from chocolate, according to her grandmother,' GR replies, and Michael looks startled, but he's obviously doing some kind of mental preparation for the flight—a mantra of *I won't be sick, I won't be sick*—and doesn't pursue the statement. I order my own toast and coffee, and join the discussion on the day's patients.

Today's first patient is a woman in her early forties with ovarian cysts. A laparoscopy on a previous visit included a biopsy and the cysts are not cancerous, but the ovaries are sufficiently affected for the woman to need both removed.

'How is she handling the idea?' I ask, knowing that, in losing both her ovaries, the woman will also lose her oestrogen production.

GR sighs.

'That's one of the few problems associated with the service,' he says, taking off his glasses and rubbing a hand across his face in a gesture that's becoming familiar. 'If she lived here in town, there could easily be a four-week delay between when I suggest surgery and when she's actually booked to have it, but during that time, if she was worried or anxious about anything, she'd know she could make an appointment to see me.'

He slips his glasses back into place, pushes them up with his forefinger, sits back for the waitress to set down his food, then continues.

'You know I consult here in town on Fridays—actually, I consult one week and operate the next. But I'm here, so patients in town know they can contact me relatively easily at least once a week. And although I tell the country patients to phone me if they're worried, or want to discuss something, they're a breed of people who "don't like to make a fuss", so, of course, they don't.'

He sounds sufficiently perturbed about this for me to feel a twinge of sympathy. Dangerous in the circumstances.

I think about the woman—the comfort being that these days there are any number of hormone replacement therapies she can try.

'You'll put her on HRT?'

'I'll definitely suggest it,' he says, but he's frowning as he says it and I can guess what's bothering him.

'I know the US study suggested it increased the chance of breast cancer, but I read a lot about that study and couldn't see anything in where they looked at other predisposing issues in the women who were taking it.'

He's tackling his gargantuan breakfast—cholesterol-laden bacon, eggs, sausages, and he has a go at me about chocolate!—while I'm talking, and kind of nods as if willing to hear what else I have to say.

'My GP back in Brisbane is a woman in her fifties who's been on it for years. I asked her what she thought and she said she was continuing to take it herself and when or if she got breast cancer, what would she blame—the fact her mother had it, or that she has two glasses of wine every night, or HRT, because all are predisposing factors? She said she couldn't do anything about the heredity and didn't intend doing anything about her alcohol consumption, and as she wasn't yet ready to give up a very enjoyable sex life, why stop taking HRT?'

At this stage Michael chokes on his tea—there must be bones in it—while GR glances around the room, no doubt to see if anyone has fallen off their chair because, once again, excitement has caused my voice to rise—just a little.

My toast arrives and I plough into it, then Michael, who's been looking puzzled since the choking exercise, asks, 'What's HRT got to do with a woman's sex life? Do women lose their libido after menopause?'

I give him a scathing look.

'No doubt, like most male students, you went to the pub when women's health lectures were on. A regular supply of oestrogen does improve a woman's libido but, more importantly for most women, oestrogen keeps the tissues in the vagina soft and well lubricated. This is essential if older women are to continue to enjoy sex.'

'So it's a far bigger issue than the uncomfortable side-effects of menopause like hot flushes and mood swings,' GR says, and I'm not sure if he's agreeing with me or asking a question. A puzzle which is solved when he adds, 'I might have to rethink my stand on women O and G specialists. You're quite right—a woman like your grandmother, for instance, would be far more likely to speak to another woman about that side of HRT benefit than she would to a man.'

My grandmother? Taking HRT to stay moist? The climbing-through-the-window conversation last night offered too much information—now this?

I look suspiciously at GR, sure there's a hidden quirk hovering around his lips. He's winding me up—he has to be—though now I remember thinking how attractive Gran looked last night, and realise there's no reason why she shouldn't have an active sex life.

Which is more than I'm enjoying…

A different nurse meets us at Gilgudgel, but I guess that's always going to be the way. Whoever is on duty, but least busy, is probably sent.

Michael heads straight for the theatre. GR tells me he's going to check on Wendy, and as he doesn't tell me I can't tag along, I go with him. She's feeding the baby as we knock and enter her room.

'Dr Prentice. Sister told me you'd be here today. My scar's healing beautifully, so is it OK if I leave hospital?'

'And what will you do if I say yes?' he asks, moving closer to examine the infant. 'Get on a horse and start moving those cattle of yours?'

'Of course not,' she assures him. 'I'll drive the truck. That's not very hard. All I have to do is pack up the camp and drive some way down the road then set up the new camp. The cattle don't travel far.'

I can feel GR's indecision, but as it's only two days since she had the Caesar there's no way he can discharge her yet. So I'm surprised again—when doesn't this man surprise me?—when he says, 'I'd prefer you to stay in for another few days, but as long as you're close enough to town to come straight in if anything happens—any bleeding, or any sign of infection—I suppose you can go. And you'll have to keep the wound clean and change the dressings yourself.'

Wendy's nodding enthusiastically.

'Sister's already told me how important it is. I can do all that, and I'll be really careful. I don't want little Wade here to be an only child.'

She smiles down at the infant in her arms, who's finished feeding and is now asleep with his little milky lips parted slightly.

So-o-o cute! I am totally hooked on new babies.

'Stay here until I finish operating,' GR tells her. 'I'll come back and check your wound then, and we'll decide when I see it.'

'You know how big this truck is, the one she's talking about driving?' I ask as we walk away. 'As well as the gear for their camp, they carry spare horses and possibly a motorbike, horse tack, horse feed, water, fuel.'

GR nods.

'But the camp can't move on until she's back with them, and the cattle have been cooped up for three days now, so will have eaten out whatever grass there was when they were yarded,' he reminds me. 'The family's livelihood depends on them keeping moving at the moment. We just have to trust she'll be careful, and anyway, with the cattle feeding, they won't travel more then ten or fifteen k. a day so she's within easy driving distance of the hospital if she needs to come back in.'

'You thought of all that while you stood there smiling at her?'

'You have to think differently out here, Blue,' he says—with no smile for me, I might add. 'Though I would have thought you'd know that. Rosebud must be one of the most isolated cattle properties in the state.'

'Just about,' I agree, and for a fleeting instant I get a wave of nostalgia for the place. Then I remember the heat and the flies, clouds of them, zooming in after rain, flapping around your ears and eyes and nose, making your arm ache with the Aussie salute—hand waved in front of face to keep them away—and tell myself nostalgia is one thing, reality another.

Only one patient to see in Gilgudgel today, and she's a woman who's having trouble conceiving.

'I saw Dr Prentice last month and he wants me to go across to the coast to see a fertility expert, but he says my husband would have to go as well, and he won't.'

'Because he can't get away from work?'

The young woman, Julie Barker, shakes her head, and presses her lips together as if to prevent bad stuff coming out.

'He's unemployed,' she says.

I feel a wave of pity for the young couple—wanting a baby but unable to afford a trip to the coast.

'You know you can apply for money to cover your fuel costs driving over there. The hospital office can give you the form to complete. And if you see the specialist at the hospital, the consultation and treatment will be free.'

Julie is not appeased by this information and finally the words she's been holding back come flying out.

'It's not the money—we can afford to go.'

Sympathy wasted!

'He doesn't want to go because he doesn't want to do the test. He says it can't be anything to do with him, he's fine and so's his sperm, and if I start telling people there's something wrong with him he'll leave me.'

And would that be so disastrous? That's my first thought as I contemplate this man. My second is that he needs a good slap about the head, but I'm more diplomatic to Julie.

'Some men feel taking sperm-count tests threatens their masculinity. Perhaps, if he's unemployed, he's already feeling stress about not being able to get a job and provide you with a more comfortable life.'

Julie gives a snort of disbelief.

'He loves being unemployed,' she says. 'It means he can lie on the couch all day and watch TV, or meet his mates in the pub.'

And you're worried about him leaving you? I think, but, as I don't know anything about marriage and find other people's relationships totally confusing, I don't say it.

'Does he want a child? Perhaps he's saying he doesn't want to do the tests because deep down he's not certain the pair of you should be having a child right now.' This doesn't sound quite right, so I add, 'Given that he's unemployed.'

'Oh, he wants a kid. All his friends have kids, and they're all unemployed as well. You get more benefits with kids.'

And no doubt it affirms his masculinity—see what I sired!

I grind a little tooth enamel off, strain my lips keeping back the words I'd like to say, and search back through Julie's file to see what GR did when he reached this impasse with her.

According to his notes, he's examined her and can find no physical reason for her not conceiving. On a previous visit, he suggested she keep a temperature chart to determine her ovulation pattern and her most fertile time. A note, in GR's strong, distinctive handwriting. 'Her husband didn't like her doing this—said it was stupid!' The dot under the exclamation mark has been dug in so hard he's practically made a hole in the paper.

So the noble GR experienced a similar frustration to what I'm going through now.

However, this isn't helping Julie.

'I think you're just going to have to get tough with him,' I tell her. 'Tell him if he wants kids he's going to *have* to go across to the coast with you. This isn't medical advice, but maybe you can shock him into going. Suppose you said something like, if he doesn't want kids, then you may as well stop having sex.'

'Stop having sex? Tell him we have to stop having sex? He'd kill me.'

Oh, boy! Is she for real? Have I gone too far?

'Literally? Is he violent?'

Julie actually smiles and shakes her head.

'Darren? Nah! He's too lazy to be violent.'

'So he wouldn't really kill you?'

'Nah, but he'd be cranky and he'd probably yell, and when he's had a few beers he'd think he can have it anyway.'

I don't think this is quite the time to point out such

behaviour is classified as rape. As I said, other people's relationships are a mystery to me.

'Well, maybe we should forget about the no-sex idea, but you need to find some way to show him you're serious about wanting him to make that trip to the coast. Go and stay with a friend or family if he gives you a hard time.'

'Leave him? But who'd look after him? Who'd cook his meals and do his washing? I couldn't do that to Darren.'

I'd like to tell her that all grown men should be able to cook and wash and look after themselves, but she'd probably wonder what planet I'd dropped from to be even thinking such a bizarre thought. Women's lib has been a long time coming in some sections of the community!

'So, how did you get on with Julie?' GR asks when we're back in the plane heading to our next port of call.

Suspicion flares.

'How did you know I saw Julie?'

He turns and smiles, making those lines deepen in his cheeks and crinkle at the corners of his eyes. It's a beautiful smile and, although it's causing little fluttering feelings in my stomach, I wish he'd use it more often.

'We always see Julie. She's the most optimistic person I know, always certain that this time, when she sees the specialist, he or she will come up with some way she can get pregnant without Darren having to be involved in anything that might in any way threaten his masculinity. I've even offered to arrange the sperm count from Gilgudgel, but when I explained to Julie what he'd have to do, she went pink, looked shocked and assured me Darren couldn't possibly do that.'

'Well, I think it's probably a good thing he's not producing more little Darrens,' I respond bitchily—it must be because I'm still squirmy from the smile, because this is the kind of terrible, judgmental remark I hate when other people make it. And GR obviously agrees it was out of order as the eyebrow rises and mild reproof is written all over his face.

The rest of the day passes without incident, and I'm beginning to realise that, apart from the difference between country and city patients, it's much like the work I'd be doing back in Brisbane.

Until we get to my last patient of the day at Amberton, a very pregnant Melanie Webster who has come in for an ultrasound.

'Did you have one earlier in the pregnancy?' I ask, and she grins at me.

'This *is* earlier in the pregnancy and, honestly, I'm eating well, but not overeating, and no junk food—as if that's possible out here.'

'Not from the outback, then,' I say as I feel my way across her belly, wondering if I'm imagining things.

'No, I was you three years ago,' she says, still smiling though now, no doubt, because she's enjoying my reaction. 'First year O and G registrar, sent out here, met this gorgeous guy on the flight out. He was going on to Mount Isa to collect a new vehicle then drive it back to his property which is about forty k. from here. Not that he spent much time on it over the next six months. He was too busy commuting to Bilbarra. Then I gave up the job and married him.'

'Which didn't please GR one bit,' I finish for her.

'GR—oh, you mean Gregor?' She stopped smiling and shook her head. 'I wasn't the first so, yes, he was really cranky, especially as he'd kind of earmarked the registrar before me as suitable wife material for himself. So you can imagine how he felt when I defected from the service to be a housewife on a cattle property. Not that he said anything much. Just a barrage of quiet disapproval washing my way for the month I spent working out my notice. That's one of the reasons I haven't had a scan before this, but…'

She hesitates and looks up at me, her blue eyes wary and yet excited. I tuck away the bit of info about the second registrar for consideration later. In his account, surely registrar number two made a play for him? Was that just talk on his part? Blaming her to hide his own weakness? Did he fall in love with her and get rejected? Maybe GR's conversation with Gran was just that—conversation. No truth in it at all.

However, I can't give that the consideration it deserves right now because something weird's happening here.

'But now you had to come because you can feel, and no doubt you've listened and can hear, more than one heartbeat?'

Her smile returned.

'I'm right, aren't I? There's more than one baby in there?'

I nod, but I'm confused as well. I'm pretty sure there can't be five—they move around a bit, tiny foetuses—but I know there are more than two.

'Let's do the scan,' I tell her. 'Then we'll know for sure.'

I walk with her to the X-ray room, pleased small hospitals now have ultrasound equipment.

The nurse—I think she's Ellen but Edenvale was a Helen so I might have it wrong—smears jelly on the distended belly, and as I pass the little instrument—ultrasounds send bursts of high-frequency sound waves into the body—over Melanie's abdomen, we're all watching the screen and counting the fluttering shapes.

'There are definitely three,' the nurse says, pointing to three distinct shapes.

'And another behind them,' Melanie says, so excited she tries to sit up. 'Oh, dear heaven, I'm having quads.'

Hopefully, I think to myself, knowing how difficult it is to carry multiple births to term—or even close to term.

But Melanie knows this as well as I do, which is possibly why she's now swearing quietly to herself and crying, but still looking pleased.

'You realise this changes the whole outlook of your pregnancy,' I tell her, as I make sure some of the images have been saved and can now be printed out. Boy, is that photograph going to be a surprise for the expectant father! 'Let's clean you up and we'll go back to the consulting room and talk about it.'

'Talk? I may never be able to talk again! And what's Angus going to say? The shock'll kill him. I'd vaguely sounded him out on twins and he thought that quite a good idea, thinking it would save me an extra pregnancy as he's always wanted two kids. But four?'

We're walking back to the consulting room, and I see her shoulders slump, and know she's gone from the high of finding out to a state of fearfulness. I guess, as a doctor who's studied O and G, she knows the chances of delivering four healthy babies are slim. The chances of delivering four full-term babies are non-existent, but nature's clever enough to compensate, and the lungs of multiple foetuses develop at a faster rate than those in a single pregnancy.

All this information is rattling through my mind while I escort Melanie back from X-ray.

Further down the passageway a patient is wheeled out of Theatre. I know GR only had one op so he should be available. First I settle Melanie in a chair, send Ellen or

Helen for a cup of tea to help ease the patient's shock, then explain to Melanie I think we need G—Gregor involved in the rest of the consultation.

She looks a little apprehensive, then admits he has more experience than the pair of us put together and agrees. I excuse myself and scuttle off to find him because I want to explain who the patient is before he sees her. After all, she's one of the reasons he's so against women O and G specialists, and I don't want him telling her it serves her right, or rehashing old annoyances.

'Ah, on time for once, Blue!' he says, as we meet outside the operating suite. He's taken off his theatre gear, but the cap has mussed his hair and I'm momentarily diverted by an urge to smooth it down. To feel its texture. Is it rough or silky?

Get with the programme here, Hillary!

'No, I'm not on time—I mean, I'm not finished. In fact, that's what I came to tell you—that we're going to be late—so do we have to let Dave know, or just leave him waiting?'

'The pilot always waits—why wouldn't he?'

Of course.

GR's frown gathers and the grey eyes do a stern look behind the glasses, but any look from those eyes is now notching my heart rate higher, so I try to concentrate on his collar as I explain.

'Melanie Reid? Having quads?' He's even more disbelieving than Melanie and I were, which is saying something.

'Actually, she's Melanie Webster now. I think she's still in shock at the moment, though she knew there were more than one. The problem is, how do we monitor her from here on. She's fifteen weeks and huge, and should really be seen every fortnight from now through to twenty weeks, then weekly if at all possible, but we're only here six-weekly, and there's no other doctor in town at the moment. Though Ellen was saying the hospital expects to get a new appointee before long, but even if that happens, he or she will be barely past internship so I don't know how effective he or she will be, or how aware of subtle pregnancy-induced changes—'

GR touches my shoulder, which effectively stops my rush of words, mainly because my mouth dries up immediately!

'Calm down, we'll handle it,' he says, his voice so soft I barely hear the words. Shifting my attention from his collar to his face, I catch a glimpse of a smile as soft as the words, and I know what I'm feeling isn't purely physical.

Great—I go from being dumped by Pete, when bells rang and whistles sounded in his life, to falling for a man who wants a tall brunette. With the help of hair dye I could manage the brunette part!

Do you think twenty-seven and a half is too old to start growth hormones?

By the time I've handled the daunting revelation of my weakness for the boss, and told myself not to be stupid about the growth hormones, GR's moved on, and is whistling his way down the corridor as if his ex-registrar being pregnant with quads is the best news he's ever heard.

I arrive back at the consulting room in time to hear him say, 'Well, you never did things by half-measures, did you, Mel?'

He bends to kiss her, and the kiss, added to the shortening of her name, makes me reassess this patient. Tall, brunette, probably fairly quiet and self-contained. Probably never wore really high-heeled sandals, and probably never fell over!

Did he earmark her as a potential wife?

I decide I hate her, but I've never had a patient having quads before so will have to put personal considerations aside.

'You know all we're going to tell you, about taking things easy—from now on, I mean, Mel—eating well, following a balanced diet, making sure you take iron, folate and other micronutrients. In fact, I'll speak to the dietician at Bilbarra and get her to send you a diet chart and list of supplements. I want your blood pressure checked at least weekly and your urine tested—you can probably take home some test strips and do it yourself—just as often. And any changes in anything—and I mean *anything*, Mel—you phone me or Blue here immediately.'

'Blue? You call this poor woman Blue? Don't you realise she's probably grown up hating that name? You haven't improved one little bit, Gregor Prentice. In fact, sometimes I wonder if you became an O and G specialist because you enjoy seeing women suffer.'

I feel like applauding Melanie for her defence, but I'm too worried about sending her back to an isolated property to bother with what GR calls me.

'How big is your place?' I ask her. 'Are there other women out there?'

Melanie smiles. 'Only my mother-in-law, two sisters-in-law and various workers' wives, one of whom is a nurse. It's a big spread.'

'And her husband has a plane so he can fly her across to the Isa or down to Bilbarra if there's any sign of trouble.' GR adds further assurance, then turns back to Melanie.

'But monitoring your health will be up to you, Mel. You're trained and capable of doing it, but you'll need a lot of emotional strength as well so you can judge your body with as much detachment as you would a patient's.'

Melanie nods, then straightens in her chair.

'I won't take any risks, Gregor. But I'd like regular check-ups with you as back-up. Do you still go to Merriwee? That's not much further for me to travel to than Amberton. Is it OK for me to see you there as well?'

'Good idea. We'll be there in a fortnight.' He reads through the notes I've made. 'You'll be seventeen weeks, then twenty-one when we come back to Amberton. I think by then you and your husband should have decided where you're going to have those babies because the less travelling you do after that the better. In fact, we might change our schedule to come to Amberton a week earlier, because from twenty weeks you should be near a hospital with specialist care.'

'What about cervical suturing? Isn't that used to help prevent onset of premature labour in multiple births?' Mel suggests.

'Or for women with a history of premature delivery,' GR reminds her. 'Yes, it's possible you'll need that, but I wouldn't be happy doing it then sending you back to the property. I'd rather, if that has to happen, you're within easy reach of a hospital.'

Melanie sighs.

'Why didn't I think of all this stuff before I fell in love?' she says, but there's enough fondness in her smile for me to feel a twinge of envy. Here's a woman who came to Bilbarra, just as I have, and found true love and happiness.

'Don't worry about her,' I hear GR say. 'She gets lost in her head.'

Indignant that he's using Gran's phrase already, I snort and say, 'I was thinking that very few people would consider the possibility of having quads before they fall in love.'

'Which, for the survival of the human species, is probably just as well,' he says, but he smiles as he says it, and I'm not only lost in my head but in my heart as well.

Thoughts of the mother I never knew send a cold shiver down my spine.

CHAPTER SIX

THIS new development keeps me quiet for the entire trip home. Because of the drama with Melanie, we're late leaving Amberton and, apart from explaining why we're late to Dave and Michael, GR's also silent.

No doubt worrying how to monitor Melanie's health long distance.

'Michael, will you drop Hillary back at the hospital?' he asks as we all disembark.

His use of my first name shocks me somewhat and, though I'm pleased, I'm also suspicious. Did Melanie's remonstrance cause the change? Does she have so much influence over him?

This is not good thinking! I can't possibly be jealous of a woman who's not only happily married but is pregnant with quads by another man.

I'm mulling over these things as we drive towards town when Michael breaks the silence I now expect from him when we're travelling.

'He's going to be late for dinner and Lydia will give him hell.'

'Lydia Dustbin,' I say automatically, though my antennae are on full alert for more information.

'Lydia Dustbin?' Michael repeats, clearly at a loss.

'Old knock-knock joke. Didn't you drive your family nuts with knock-knock jokes? Knock knock, who's there, Lydia, Lydia who, Lydia Dustbin.'

Michael doesn't seem much wiser when I finish explaining, and I can sense his relief when we arrive at the hospital.

'I wouldn't mention the knock-knock joke to her,' he says. 'Lydia takes herself very seriously.'

'Oh!'

I wait for more information, like why I'm likely to be mentioning anything to her. Is the GR-Lydia relationship so close I'll see a lot of her? But waiting for more information from Michael is like waiting at the bus stop for a moon rocket.

I have to ask.

'Who is she? The boss's girlfriend? Lover?'

OK, that last is going beyond what's valid employer-employee questioning, but I couldn't help myself.

'She's the local mayor—not that they have mayors out here. They have shire councils, and she's the chairman.'

Michael stops and turns, obviously expecting me to get out of the car. No way! I'm not Gran's granddaughter for nothing.

'And?' I prompt.

'That's all,' Michael says, squirming uncomfortably.

'So the boss is having dinner with her to report on the state of the footpath outside the hospital? Or discuss the quality of the water? Come on, Michael, tell me more!'

'I don't like gossiping,' he says, and I look at him in frank disbelief.

'You *are* a doctor?' I ask, maybe overdoing the incredulous act a wee bit. 'You did train and work in a hospital? And you don't like gossiping? Michael, you can't survive in a hospital system without gossip. You'd never learn anything if you didn't indulge, just a little, in the talk of who's doing what to whom. Besides, I wouldn't call what we're discussing gossip—it's more information-sharing. You know the boss doesn't like working with women registrars so give me a break here—help me out. Fill me in on who's who in his life so I don't make any gross *faux pas*.'

Michael looks how I feel when I'm sitting in the waiting room at the dentist—kind of pained, and apprehensive, with a big dose of panic thrown in.

'I really don't know anything. I've only been here a couple of months myself. All I know is Gregor goes to Lydia's for dinner every Tuesday night.'

'Maybe she's a friend of his mother's,' I say, because although I know GR's social life is nothing to do with me—or ever likely to be my business—I can't help feeling overwhelmingly jealous of this woman, in a way I didn't for an instant feel over Pete's Claudia.

It must be because of the revelation I had earlier. Jealousy must be a byproduct of infatuation.

I'm so busy working out what's happening to me I miss Michael's reply, but I did hear the snort of laughter that prefaced it.

'*What* did you say?'

'I said I wish my mother had friends that gorgeous. You'll meet Lydia eventually as she's often around the hospital, but for your information she's a tall, elegant, thirtyish brunette with legs that look stunning in a mini. She's probably the most glamorous shire councillor in the entire country.'

I'm sorry I asked. I should have known. My legs don't look bad in a mini—but stunning?

I growl at Michael and clamber out of his car, then realise the lights aren't on in the old quarters. Has Gran gone home?

I go from wondering when she's leaving to feeling sorry for myself that she's gone in a heartbeat, but once inside I find a note, which details what she's organised for my dinner—a microwave oven has appeared in the kitchen area—and where she's gone.

'To catch up with an old friend,' the note explains, and I realise that, in between climbing in and out of windows to see Grandad, she would almost certainly have made friends in town. And Gran being the kind of person she is, she'd have kept in touch with them.

I'm starving so I pull the bowl of pasta she's prepared out of the fridge and bung it in the microwave, wash my hands while it's zapping then carry it to the little table. No, I don't find the tablecloth she's borrowed from the hospital—I'm a slob and I'm quite happy to eat off bare wood.

I'm also grumpy and tell myself it's with Gran for going off and leaving me alone on only her second night in town, but in fact it's the information Michael shared so reluctantly that's niggling at me. Lydia Dustbin's long, sexy legs.

Actually, he didn't say sexy, I remind myself, but that doesn't help.

I have a shower, then go through my clothes so I'm prepared for another early start in the morning. I find my jeans, freshly laundered by Gran who has a washing fetish, and, providing I avoid any excessive indulgences tonight, I should still be able to fit into them tomorrow.

Tomorrow? Has GR told me where we go tomorrow?

I can't recall any details and though I've got a schedule, he usually fills me in on the next day's programme on the flight back to Bilbarra. Of course, worrying about Melanie could have distracted him.

And no doubt he was thinking of his dinner date with you know who. I check the schedule—two towns I've never heard of—then go to bed, edgy and irritable, though

I sleep soundly enough not to hear Gran return whenever she comes in.

She's up, of course, when I haul myself out of bed next morning and make my way, grumpier than ever, towards the bathroom.

Once I've had a quick shower, I'm a slightly nicer person, so I ask her how her evening went.

'Oh, fine,' she says. 'I've made toast. Do you want some?'

I glance out the louvres, but there's no vehicle pulling up.

'I guess so,' I tell her, wondering if Michael's been given permanent chauffeur duties. It's surely not possible for GR to be late.

Michael arrives as I finish the toast.

'Gregor asked me to collect you,' he says, as I hurry out to the car.

'Yesterday?'

Michael looks puzzled.

'I didn't collect you yesterday.'

I grit my teeth at the literal interpretation, but it's not worth explaining that what I really wanted to know was when this decision was made. Not that it matters. There was no reason why the boss should be driving me around when he has an underling in Michael who could do it.

'I'm sorry, but we don't have time to stop at the roadhouse,' Michael explains as we roar past it. 'Wednesday's always a long day, so the boss hates late starts.'

'And what if I hadn't had breakfast?' I demand.

Michael grins.

'Tough buns!' he says, using a phrase I'd used at him that first day. 'In that case you'd know how I feel most mornings. Starving, yet afraid to eat.'

'Don't you think you'd feel better if you did eat something?'

'I've tried that. It was so disastrous I won't be doing it again. I'm OK if I eat when we get to the first hospital. The food has time to settle before the next flight.'

My stomach squirms as Michael continues to describe his intestinal problems, and I'm sorry I had the toast. But we're at the airport now, and Dave's flying us again. At least I think it's Dave but just say 'Hi' in case I'm wrong. GR's waiting by the plane and, thanks to not stopping on the way, we're right on time.

'Morning!' I say, and smile brightly at him.

He frowns as if trying to remember who I am, then nods absently, still frowning.

There's a little bit of my heart that doesn't like the frown. It's fretting over it so, of course, I can't ignore it.

'Something weighty on your mind?'

He looks startled, then turns to Dave—or maybe Bob—and nods to say we're ready to go.

'I'll need you to assist today.'

This statement is delivered over his shoulder many minutes later when we're in the air, heading towards Caribunya.

'It's a hysterectomy, and I'm not certain yet but I think I might have to remove Mrs Jackman's ovaries as well. The left almost certainly, I'm not so sure about the right.'

So maybe he did have something weighty on his mind!

I ask all the right questions, about the patient's age—thirty-seven—and GR's diagnosis—endometrial polyps and lesions from an earlier operation.

Lesions, which are like internal scar tissue, can occur after any surgery, and in the abdomen can cause problems to other organs, in worst-case scenarios strangling the lower intestine.

'That seems unfair, that something to relieve symptoms earlier should cause more problems now,' I say, but garner no response from GR.

So we arrive at Caribunya and although this is only my third official day on the job, already the routine seems normal. The drive from airport to town, the first glimpse of the hospital, meeting different nursing staff, occasionally the local hospital superintendent or a local GP.

I meet Mrs Jackman before Michael does the pre-med, then GR and I both see patients while Michael is checking on allergies and deciding on the best anaesthesia for this particular patient.

Then we're off to Theatre and I realise operating with GR is a whole new experience.

He's good—very good, in fact—swift, precise, efficient movements that I'd love to emulate. One day, I tell myself. One day, I'll be the best O and G specialist in Queensland—maybe the world! Women will fly in—

'Just shift that clamp.'

I bring my mind back to the job, but operating with someone means standing very close to them and, try as I may to blot out the physical manifestations of being close to him, they are too strong to ignore altogether.

He points out the lesions, which have certainly distorted the beautiful symmetry of Mrs Jackman's internal organs, and, under orders, I snip and seal and probe and tie, until he's satisfied he's eradicated the problem.

'Great job,' Michael says as GR steps back to allow me to close. 'You said two hours and you were spot on.'

I glance up in time to see GR nod in satisfaction, but when he turns to me there's a frown creasing the only bit of skin I can see—his forehead.

Once the wound is dressed, Michael and the theatre runner wheel the patient out, the theatre sister gathers up the instruments and bustles off, while I follow GR to the small room where we strip off our Theatre garb, hurling the soiled clothes into the bin. You get used to shared changing rooms early in your training so we're as unself-conscious about being in the same room in our underwear as kids in kindergarten.

Until our arms collide mid-throw—well, he's throwing and I'm pulling on my T-shirt. It's a very small room for two people to be using—and we both stop. I stop because the unexpected physical contact affects me in the way this man's been affecting me since the first handshake. I don't know why he stops until he turns, grips my shoulders, tugs me close and kisses me.

Hard, hot, angry almost, but, oh, if his hands had zap-ping power, it's nothing to what his lips can do. I'm float-ing somewhere in the air, my body so sensitised I can feel air molecules brushing against my skin.

I also feel I'm teetering on the edge of an avalanche. One false move and I'll be swept into oblivion.

Self-preservation makes me pull away and frown at him, then remember that the best form of defence is at-tack.

'No wonder you don't like working with women reg-istrars if you can't keep your lips to yourself.'

'Damn it, Blue!' he grumbles, frowning right back at me. 'It's got nothing to do with why I prefer not to have women registrars. It's you. Being anywhere in your vicin-ity is like having a live wire flipping around in the air. Right from when I first shook hands with you, something sizzled along my nerves. What's with you?'

'What's with me? It's you that's doing it,' I tell him, sure my lips must be swollen to twice their usual size, so electric was the kiss. '*I* don't zap people every time I touch them.'

'No?' he growls. 'Well, you're zapping me and I want it to stop. It's ridiculous. We don't know each other—hell, we probably wouldn't like each other if we did—so this has got to be some strange pheromone reaction, nothing more than a glitch we have to learn to live with.'

'By kissing in the changing room?' I retort, upset because he used the word I've been using in my mind—calling whatever is happening a glitch as if that somehow minimises it. 'What was that about?'

'I don't know. It must have been because you touched me. You made me do it.'

This is a grown man, standing there in his underwear, bleating that it's my fault?

'I made you do it?'

OK, so I'm bleating, too, but this isn't your everyday post-operative situation. This is something so bizarre I don't have either the mental or physical strength to cope with it.

'Well, I've never done it before,' he complains, backing away and pulling on his trousers. 'I've never even wanted to do it before, or considered I might ever even think about doing it before, or—'

'I get the picture,' I tell him, interrupting before the list gets any longer. 'This was a one-off for you, too.'

He's got his shirt on now, and is slipping buttons into buttonholes. I don't tell him he's got them wrong. In fact, I enjoy this evidence of his confusion. If I wasn't wearing a T-shirt I'd be buttoning wrong for sure.

'I'm almost engaged,' he adds, as if that's the clincher in the argument. A vivid picture of a dustbin on long, sexy legs pops obligingly into my head, and I bite back a growl of my own.

But he's right—it's an obscure chemical glitch, that's

all, and at least now we've talked about it we can get on with ignoring it. As long as he doesn't kiss me again.

And I don't give in to any rampant desire to kiss him!

Disappointment ripples through me, and I weaken. Maybe just once, I decide, to see if it was as sensational as I thought it was.

I sneak a quick glance at his face. He's discovered the buttonhole problem and is concentrating on getting them right, so I check his lips to make sure there are no electrodes in evidence.

Then I remember my mother and the Argentinian and remind myself that surrendering to hormonal surges is *not a good idea*.

But looking at those lips…

Michael joins us at this stage and, suddenly embarrassed at my state of half-dress—and where my thoughts have taken me—I hurry into my jeans.

To all outward appearances, GR is handling this much better than I am, though I suppose I look OK on the outside, too. Inside, I'm a mess—fluttery things happening within me when I look at him, shivery things occurring when he speaks, total mental disintegration when he looks at me!

We move on to Wetherby, up in the air, short flight, touchdown. Michael is as silent as ever, GR discusses changes to next week's schedule with Dave, and I look at him in profile—GR that is, not Dave—and wonder about the perversity of chemical attraction.

By the time we arrive back at Bilbarra airfield I'm so totally confused I need time out. I manoeuvre Michael to one side and ask him to give me a lift, but GR stalls that idea, saying he needs to discuss tomorrow's programme.

'I thought, given neither of us want any involvement, we might be better off not being together any more than is absolutely necessary,' I grouch, as we head towards town. 'And, that being the case, I'm cancelling my visit to your property this weekend. Gran can go if she likes, or just drive out for a visit, but count me out.'

'Scared, Blue?' he says, flicking one of his quirky smiles in my direction.

'Don't call me Blue!' I snap, driven nearly to desperation by this situation.

He grins again.

'It's my only defence. I need to keep thinking of you that way—as a kind of a mate rather than a woman.'

'Heaven forbid you should think of me as a woman,' I tell him. 'A woman and, what's worse, a female O and G specialist in training!'

He slows and pulls off the road, takes off his glasses, rubs his eyes, puts the glasses back on again, then scratches his head.

'I'm sorry. Every time I open my mouth I make matters worse, don't I? But you've got to understand, I'm used to being in control—of my life, my work, my emotions, everything. Then you breeze into town and turn me on my ear. I can accept physical attraction exists, but not to this extent. And you don't believe it either—you said you couldn't understand your ex's bells-and-flashing-lights attraction to the woman he met.'

Well, I didn't believe it then, I consider saying, but realise it's better if he doesn't know just how close I've come to reconsidering my opinion on the subject. OK, so he's admitted feeling the same attraction I feel but, so far as I can remember, given the momentousness of the kiss, which has left sections of my brain distinctly hazy, I haven't made any admissions.

'So what do we do about your problem?' I ask. 'I've

suggested avoidance tactics. Have you anything better to offer?'

'My problem? You didn't exactly push me away when we kissed.'

'You took me by surprise,' I tell him, but I can see he doesn't believe it.

'The kiss was mutual,' he reminds me, then pauses, gazing through the windscreen as if the secrets of the universe—or even of mutual attraction—might be written up in a gum tree. 'I don't suppose you'd like a quick and very discreet affair? I don't normally proposition my registrars and casual sex isn't something I do, but, hell…'

I'm still bogged down at the 'quick and very discreet' part so don't butt in when he pauses to take off his glasses and rub his hands across his face.

Nice face…

'It might release the tension that's humming between us and everything could return to normal.'

He hesitates again and I get the feeling he was speaking the truth when he said he doesn't do it often. The man's as muddled as I am.

'I wouldn't ask,' he continues, 'but I know a lot of women these days are advocates of healthy sexual relationships without hang-ups about commitment or feelings of guilt. They treat sex in much the same way men have always treated it.'

'And you're asking if I'm one of them?' I'm startled by the request but intrigued as well, so I answer honestly. 'No, I'm not. Not that I've ever really had the option of doing it, what with being with Pete and all, but, no, I can tell you, for sure and certain, I am not an affair kind of woman—no matter how quick or discreet it is. Which, given the fact my grandmother is staying with me, is probably a good thing.'

'Pity,' he says, and disappointment that he doesn't press me on the matter—suggest ways and means of getting around the Gran situation—zooms through me.

I'm so angered by this absurd reaction—or maybe by his assumption I won't attract him for long—that whatever it is between us is purely physical, I go on the attack again.

'Pity? You were actually considering it? Didn't you say you were nearly engaged? Nice one, GR! Just how long after we end the quick and very discreet affair would you be proposing? One day? A week?'

'What did you call me?'

Hell, what did I call him? I try to think, but my mind's gone blank.

'What did it sound like?' I mumble weakly. What could I possibly have called him? Let it not be 'darling' or something equally revealing, and if it was, could a lightning bolt, please strike me *now*.

'It sounded like ''GR'',' he says, and relief floods through me.

'Oh, that,' I say. 'That's OK. That's how I think of you. I missed the Gregor part when you first introduced yourself, and the initials kind of stuck in my head.'

'Like Blue,' he muses, and because I don't want him thinking I use the initials to distance myself from him, I zero back in on an earlier bit of the conversation. The bit he conveniently didn't answer.

'Anyway, given all that guff you told Gran the other night about believing in love—how can you be ''nearly'' engaged? Surely, after waiting all this time for love, you must know whether you've found it. And if you have, why the ''nearly''?'

The fascinating tinge of colour creeps into his cheeks.

'This is different,' he mutters, then frowns at me.

'Look, I wasn't lying when I said those things to your grandmother, though I don't know why it all came out when I'd barely met the woman—'

I do—Gran does that to you.

'But I'm thirty-five and I can't help wondering if it might *not* happen for me. If what I was waiting for isn't in the grand plan that's guiding my life. Maybe fate's decided it's not for me, and I'm waiting for nothing. I have a friend here in town, a good friend, and she'd like to get married, and to tell you the truth, Blue, I'm getting tired of going home to a slow-cooker.'

'And of quick, very discreet affairs?' I can't help asking.

'No!' he says, then glares when I chuckle. 'You know perfectly well what I mean. I mean, no, I don't indulge in quick discreet affairs—or any kind of affairs. I've had relationships with women, but recently, well, living in a country town is like living in a fishbowl, so…' He pauses then smiles so radiantly it's as if a light has just flicked on in his head.

The smile stuns me, then fires frenzy along my nerves, but fortunately the effect can't be obvious because he doesn't notice, just explains the brilliant revelation he experienced to cause the smile.

'That's what this is, Blue. It's my libido reminding me just how long it is since I've had sex. It's lust, pure and simple.'

'I didn't think there was anything pure about lust, and this situation isn't exactly what I'd term simple,' I mutter, and he laughs.

'But doesn't understanding something always make it clearer?' he demands with great delight. I don't bother telling him it hasn't made it any clearer for me. It's not *that* long since I split up with Pete! Five months or so, not years and years.

'It doesn't make how to handle it easier,' I remind him. He fixes me with a certain look he gets—as if he's faced with a new species of animal life—or maybe he's just trying to read more into my words. Or maybe it's just his glasses that make him look intent and he's not thinking anything at all.

'Avoidance won't be easy, given we have to work together,' he finally says, showing me just how far off the mark I was in my guesses. I told you he isn't an easy man to read.

'So what's your solution?'

I've been the only helpful one so far in this conversation and I'm getting sick of it.

'I haven't got one,' he admits, 'so I guess we'll just have to practise self-restraint.'

'*We'll* have to practice self-restraint? It wasn't my half of *we* who initiated that kiss.'

'You responded,' he reminds me, and I refrain from comment, too embarrassed by the intensity of my response to even want to think about it.

Then suddenly he's moving closer, and another kiss seems inevitable. My heart rate accelerates so drastically I'm shaking, and my head's whirling with too much delirious anticipation to even consider not kissing him back, and my lips quiver with excitement.

Then he's talking, not kissing, and I'm so confused I barely hear the words.

But I get the sense of them. We're two mature adults—thank heaven he can't see beneath my skin, because right now I'm about as mature as a randy teenager in the throes of first love—and as such should be able to handle what is nothing more than a chemical reaction.

'So we're back with the pheromones and glitch again,' I think, then realise I've actually said it when he straightens up and frowns at me.

'Well, you have to admit that's all it can be,' he says. 'Love can't strike like a thunderbolt and zap through the nerves like lightning.'

I nod, because rationally I *do* agree with him. If people fancied themselves in love every time their pheromones got zapped, the world would be a mess. Being a living example of that kind of behaviour, I know this for a fact!

He starts the car and pulls back out on the road. I'm not sure we've solved anything, but knowing he's feeling the same electrical impulses as I am will certainly make me much more cautious.

We drive back to the hospital, only more slowly than he usually drives, and I wonder if he feels the same sense of loss—as if something special is finished—which I'm feeling.

Finished before it began…

Lights are shining through the louvres so at least Gran's at home. Maybe some normal conversation and just a little bit of grandmotherly fussing will make things right again.

Gran comes rushing down the steps as GR stops the car, arms waving to attract someone's attention. And as I'll shortly be walking into the old quarters I assume it isn't mine.

'Oh, Gregor,' she says, as he climbs out of the car. 'I've been waiting to see you. I know you'll probably call in at the hospital to see your patients, and you'd hear there anyway, but in case you didn't I thought you should know Charles is in hospital.'

Hear there? Hear what?

And who the hell is Charles?

I'm wondering these things as Gran rushes on.

'He had a fall. Silly man tried to get something off a high shelf and tipped his chair over. He put out a hand to save himself and fractured his wrist. It's been plastered and he could have gone home, but the doctor wanted to keep him in. And, anyway, it's his right hand so he'll really need some help in the house when he does come out.'

'Independent old bugger!' GR growls. 'I've been trying to convince him to get help in the house for years, but will he listen? Now he might be forced to accept someone. Thank you, Mrs Green.'

He turns away, climbs into the car and reverses across to the car park behind the hospital. I watch him disappear into the rear of the building, then turn to Gran.

'And what was that all about? Who is Charles? How do you know him? And exactly where does my boss fit into the situation?'

Gran laughs. No, it's more an embarrassed kind of giggle. And she flutters her hands in the air, then finally says, 'Charles is an old friend. He was married to Esme who nursed with me here. His family owned the property where your grandfather worked. Anyway, Esme and I kept in touch then about eight years ago they had a car accident. Esme was driving and she was killed and Charles was seriously injured and very sick for a long time. He ended up more or less permanently in a wheelchair.'

'He's the friend you visited yesterday?' I ask, remembering the blush and intrigued by the possibility of my grandmother and Charles eventually being more than friends. Was it something in the air at Bilbarra that had even middle-aged hormones twitching?

'Yes,' Gran says, recovering from her agitation and leading the way inside. 'It's a small world, isn't it?' she adds, positively glowing with goodwill. 'It turns out he's

Gregor's uncle—his mother's brother. His mother grew
up on the property, which is one of the reasons Gregor
bought it after Charles had the accident. Charles and Esme
only had one daughter and she married a city man, so it
would have passed out of the family.'

I go right off the idea of my grandmother having any
kind of a relationship with Charles. Avoiding GR whenever possible over the next six months is one thing, avoiding him for ever if his close relation ends up in a close
relationship with my nearest and dearest relative would
be impossible.

Not even the fiendish fate that's currently got me in its
sights—Pete's defection and the transfer to Bilbarra being
testament to this—could entangle me with GR for a lifetime!

I'm thinking about this, so I'm not really listening to
what Gran's saying when she says, 'Well, now Gregor's
had time to see him, I might go back over. I only left
because I wanted to catch you when you got back, to let
Gregor know. I made a nice shepherd's pie. You just need
to pop the plate in the microwave. Aren't microwaves
blissful things?'

And on this note the grandmother I thought had come
down to Bilbarra to see me—and perhaps nurture me just
a little—departs to pursue her own agenda.

Charles.

Uncle of GR.

My throat tightens and I know I'd choke on shepherd's
pie so I find a box of chocolates I was keeping for a very
special occasion and eat a couple of them. Because of
their smooth texture and ability to melt, they slide down
tight throats quite easily. To prove this theory I eat a couple more. Then, because it was a very small box and there
are only two left, I finish them off.

I'm now feeling slightly ill, so I have a shower and get into my pyjamas. I'm a class act in pyjamas. Gran sends me some for Christmas every year—ordered from a catalogue and usually featuring either hearts—I should have guessed she was a romantic before Charles entered the picture—or flowers. This year's pair is a vivid violet colour that hasn't faded in a hundred washes, and they've got hearts—big purple hearts—splashed across them.

I wander up and down the veranda, regretting the chocolates and wondering what to do about the shepherd's pie. If Gran returns and finds it in the fridge she'll be upset.

And nag.

But if I scrape it into the kitchen tidy, she's sure to see it there, even if I hide it under chocolate wrappers. No, I'd better hide the chocolate wrappers, too.

I'm wondering where the big industrial bins all hospitals have are situated, and considering a midnight dash to get rid of all the evidence, when there's a footfall on the steps outside.

Damn! She's back. Now I'll have to eat the dinner.

I decide this isn't such a bad idea as I know from experience that chocolate fullness wears off very quickly. Then GR appears, holding out his hand as if in apology for disturbing me until he catches the full glory of the pyjamas and laughs out loud.

'Well, that's certainly a better idea than avoidance,' he says when he recovers enough to speak. 'Passion-killer pyjamas. If your ex was subjected to them on a regular basis, no wonder bells and whistles happened when he met the other woman.'

I am so furious I want to stamp my feet, and possibly scream a little, or throw something. Then a better idea surfaces in my head.

'They're a turn-off, are they?' I ask, in the huskiest

voice I can manage. 'I guess that's what Gran intends when she sends me a pair each Christmas.'

I'm slinking down the veranda towards him as I speak—well, I'm going for a slink but, not having done much slinking in the past, I don't know how it's coming off. Whatever, he's seemingly riveted to the spot, which is what I want because I need to be very close.

'Passion-killers?' I repeat, just to be sure he gets the point, then I stand on tiptoe and do the one thing I was determined not to do.

I kiss the man.

CHAPTER SEVEN

BIG mistake! His lips join in, parting mine, his tongue explores and a zillion nerves respond with a ferocity that scares me because I feel as if I'm truly alive for the first time in twenty-seven years.

Kisses can't do this, I tell myself, still kissing because I can't stop. Can't bear the thought of not feeling the magic his touch generates in my body. His hands clasp my shoulders, steadying me but sending as many messages as his lips. I want those hands moving, exploring, touching all the acutely sensitised parts of my body he's awakened.

Underneath the passion-killers my body heats with a subversive hunger so strong that common sense and self-preservation are all but swept away.

All but!

I remember my origins and the fear that's always haunted me—that I might turn out to be like my mother after all. The kiss is kindling a desire so strong I want to tear off his clothes, and my clothes, and do something to ease the ache.

Is this how she felt?

Again and again, as Uncle Joel's wife, Jill, claims? Or just with the polo player?

I don't know, but the 'again and again' part terrifies me. If I give in once, will that be my fate?

'I need to breathe,' I whisper, and ease my body, which is practically glued to GR's, a safe distance away.

Safe? Two hundred k. might be safe. Or two thousand.

He reaches out and touches my hair, flicking his finger at a strand of it.

'Shall I tell your gran the pyjamas didn't work, or will you?' he says, the little quirk lifting the corner of his mouth in a rueful smile.

Once again the suspicion that this is a really nice man flutters through my head, but really nice plus zap-power is probably more dangerous than downright nasty.

Really nice can get a girl in trouble.

'I don't think we'll mention it,' I tell him, realising for the first time he's had his glasses on right through the kiss.

'It's a wonder the rims didn't melt,' I mutter, and he reaches up to touch the frames then laughs.

'Tell me I didn't have them on the first time I kissed you. Surely I had enough class to take them off.'

'They were off, because you were changing,' I assure him, but I have to smile. He's so obviously confused by what's happening I'm beginning to believe he really meant what he said when he talked to Gran about love. Here he is, thirty-five and still waiting for the miracle to happen. Still putting off proposing to the dustbin to give love a chance to come along.

But is love like that? Does it just happen? Might he not have to go in search of it?

I get this far then realise I don't want him searching for it. I forget my own qualms about what's happening between us and decide I want him considering whether love might not be right here. I want him considering that the glitch might be more than just a glitch.

After four days! I'm scoffing at such truly scary thoughts, and GR's talking, and I realise Gran's returned and is asking about who organises home help.

'I'd shift in myself to help him out, but I think he

should get over this independence bee he's got in his bonnet and sneaking in a proper paid helper while he's injured might be the way to do it.'

She's obviously talking about GR's Uncle Charles and GR is agreeing with her, saying he can organise the help.

'Of course you can't,' Gran tells him. 'The hours you work, it's a wonder you get time to eat and sleep. No, I'm here and not doing anything. Give me the name of the person to ring and I'll arrange it.'

Further discussion on the recalcitrant patient so my mind drifts back to the kiss, while my body relives the delicious sensations it experienced.

'We've got two Caesars booked for tomorrow at Merriwee. Do you want to do them?'

My brain snaps back to attention so suddenly it's a wonder he didn't hear it. If he's talking Caesars it must be to me, not Gran.

He's watching me, head cocked, grey eyes agleam, knowing damn well he's caught me lost in my head again.

'Caesars? We do Caesars? I didn't think we delivered babies unless it was an emergency. Are these optional? Have the women asked for a Caesarean delivery? Do you do them on request?'

If he's surprised by my flow of questions he doesn't show it, though Gran, who's walked away, is chuckling to herself.

'We do them for women who are at risk in a normal delivery. One of tomorrow's patients is having her third child. She broke her pelvis in an accident when she was young and the bones healed badly so they no longer have the ability to move during delivery. The second woman is having her second child. She retained the placenta after the birth of her first, and it couldn't be removed manually so had to be operated on. It's a hereditary problem so likely to happen with this second delivery. Given her history, it's easier for her to have a Caesar.'

He pauses, as if waiting for a comment, and I try to think why we're discussing this.

'So, do you want to do them?' he says, realising I've lost the conversational plot.

'I'd love to,' I tell him. 'So you'll do the consulting?'

He grins.

'If there is any,' he says. 'Merriwee has a great woman doctor who seems more than competent at handling gynaecological problems. It's one of the easiest towns we visit and, as a bonus, although we usually go on from there to Tarrayalla, there are no patients to see there so we'll have an early day.'

He grins then adds, 'That's what I came to tell you. You can shop for boots tomorrow afternoon.'

He touches his hand to his forehead, as if tipping an imaginary hat, calls goodnight to Gran, nods to me and walks, soft-footed, back along the veranda and out the door.

To say I'm confused would be understating my mental state severely. And now Gran's discovered I haven't eaten the shepherd's pie. I resign myself to this particular fate and sit down at the table—bedecked with the borrowed tablecloth—and eat.

Shepherd's pie is not good brain food. It does nothing to clear the muddle in my head.

White chocolate, now...

Fortunately, Gran has a heap of information about Charles to impart, so I don't have to contribute more than a few encouraging noises to the conversation.

A tall man with gorgeous blue eyes meets us at the airfield at Merriwee.

'All the animals in town healthy, are they, Tom?' GR

asks him, then introduces me to Tom Fleming. 'Husband of Dr Anna Fleming and local veterinary surgeon.'

'The animals are healthy but I'm not so sure about Anna. She never complains, but I know she's overdoing things. She's been here over twelve months without a break, and though the Health Department keep promising her a locum, there never seems to be one available.'

Tom's leading us towards his car as he talks, and continues airing his concerns as we head for town.

'She'll never get a locum if she waits for the department to appoint one,' GR tells him. 'She has to just announce she's taking holidays and that's that.'

'Can you see Anna voluntarily leaving Merriwee without a doctor?' Tom says. 'She loves this town.'

'I gather, as you're doing the driving duties, you have a plan,' GR says.

Tom grins.

'I do indeed. Remember on your last visit you were talking about the O and G conference at Surfers Paradise in May? You were saying there were places set aside for rural and remote GPs to attend so they could hear people speak on the latest developments in your field.'

GR nods.

'Well, she'd really love to go. It's still six weeks away so there's time to arrange a locum, and I thought if you put in a recommendation for her to attend, she'd kind of be forced to go, and we could have a holiday while we're there.'

'I can easily do that, but I'll explain she'll need locum cover out here when I speak to the department. That might carry more weight than her applications.'

Tom reaches out and claps him on the shoulder.

'Thanks, mate,' he says, and the heartfelt tone and familiar touch make me realise they *are* mates, these two. Either recent friends, or maybe going way back. And suddenly I feel a sense of loss.

Home-schooled by Gran, I don't have friends who go way back. Even at university, I met up with Pete so early in the course I didn't make many female friends there. Acquaintances by the bucketload, but friends?

GR would make a nice friend…

Tom stops at the hospital and we disembark. He toots the horn as he drives away, obviously wanting to appear totally uninvolved with the team.

'You OK, Blue?'

I'm so startled by the question I look up and see concern in GR's eyes. It disturbs me more than the usual teasing glint.

'Why wouldn't I be?' That's me on the attack again. 'If you must know, I was thinking about the operations—about two sets of parents anxiously awaiting the births of their babies.'

I can practically feel my underwear singeing even though I have my fingers crossed behind my back.

Anna Fleming is tall, blonde, beautiful and utterly charming to boot. All the things I'm not. GR chats easily to her, Michael gazes adoringly at her, and she breaks down my resistance the moment she says, 'What glorious hair. I know blonde is supposed to be a coveted colour, but it's so anaemic compared to that vibrant titian.'

I babble something in reply, then meet my two very pregnant patients and the theatre nurse.

'I'd love to assist, if that's OK,' Anna says, and I assure her she'll be welcome. Then I glance at GR, thinking that if he was operating it might be a chance to talk to Anna about the conference, but he gives just the slightest shake of his head.

I know he can't read my thoughts, but there've been so many occasions, right from when we first met, when it seems as if we're attuned to each other. Weird, that's what it is.

I explain to the women what's going to happen. They're friends and have opted to hear this information together.

'Actually,' one of them, Hope Harris, admits when the men go off to put on Theatre gear, 'we thought it might be easier for our husbands if we did it together. My husband, Michael, has been at both my previous births, but Penny's husband missed her first. He's a contract harvester and was away when she had Albert.'

Albert? Who'd ever name a tiny baby Albert? I'm thinking, as I decide to do Hope first. Then I realise Penny's husband was introduced to me as Al, so assume he's Albert, too, and tell myself not to be judgmental about babies' names.

Two beautiful, straightforward Caesarean operations later, and the population of Merriwee has risen by two. Babies born this way look so much better, I'm thinking as I peer first into Samantha's crib, then into Patrick's. They are pink and gorgeous, having been born without the stress of passing down the birth canal with their mothers screaming abuse at the men who landed them in the predicament.

It doesn't always happen—but in most cases, at some stage in a delivery, the woman remembers whose fault it is she's where she is. In rational moments she's probably prepared to take at least fifty per cent of the blame, but during labour it is *always* the man who's responsible.

Samantha's eyes open and their blueness mesmerises me.

'Did you know before you opted to specialise in O and G that new babies broke you up?'

GR has appeared beside me, and obviously registered the soggy tissue I'm clasping in my hand.

'I can't help it—they're so perfect,' I tell him, refusing to pretend I'm not always overwhelmed by the newborn perfection. 'And the answer's no, anyway. I went into it because my mother died in childbirth. I know that doesn't happen often these days, but she was neglectful of her health and it happened to her. I suppose, growing up knowing that I'd been, if only accidentally, responsible for her death, I wanted to do something to make amends.'

Silence from my companion. A silence that stretches so long I turn from the babies to look at him.

'What?' I demand, and when he doesn't reply I snap at him. 'I don't over-sentimentalise it, it just happened. You asked for a reason and I gave it.'

He shakes his head.

'I'm sorry—it was just the last thing I expected you to say. I did wonder about your closeness to your grandmother, but never for a moment imagined—'

'That I didn't have a mother?' I shrug. I'm OK with this stuff—it's just that babies make me cry. 'I don't have a father either. Well, not one who knows about me. But I've done OK. Gran brought me up, and Grandad was wonderful—even Uncle Joel did his bit.'

'Of course,' GR says, but he still looks shell-shocked.

'There's no reason why you would know any of this,' I tell him. 'Apart from the fact your parents had a happy marriage, I don't know much about you.'

Actually, now I think about it, I do—I know about his Uncle Charles and dead Aunt Esme—but I battle on.

'We're colleagues, that's all.'

But he shakes his head, and bends over to have a look at the babies.

'I can understand why you'd avoid casual affairs,' he says quietly. 'I'm sorry I was so flippant as to suggest it.'

Now *I'm* shell-shocked. Why does he have to be so *nice*?

And since when is 'nice' bad? I ask myself, much later, when we're heading back to Bilbarra for my first afternoon off. It's already after two so it won't be much of an afternoon, but I'm looking forward to seeing more of the town than the road to the airfield.

The plane rises, steadies out at its designated altitude and Merriwee is lost behind us. I'm watching the pilot as usual, so I'm the first to react when Bob slumps forward so his head is resting against the control panel. He doesn't make a sound.

I know he sets the plane on autopilot as soon as we reach cruising altitude, so we aren't about to nosedive. I unbuckle my harness and lean forward, my arms around Bob, to unbuckle his.

'Let's get him across so his head's lying on Gregor's lap,' I say to Michael, who's shocked into helping me ease the dead weight of the pilot sideways.

The plane, suddenly smaller, seems to tilt as we move in the cabin. Gregor's grasped the situation to the extent he's breathing air into Bob's lungs while still trying to move him into a better position, but any other form of CPR is going to be close to impossible.

'I'm going to take us back to Merriwee,' I inform my fellow passengers. Michael's green but pretending he's all right, reaching forward to try to shift Bob's body so either he or Gregor can do chest compressions.

Gregor's eyes meet mine when he looks up to take a

breath. I can read a thousand questions in them, but I answer only one.

'I told you I'd flown planes like this.'

I've climbed over the seat and am balanced on Bob's legs. We'll have to come down very gently because there's no way I can get into a harness. Behind me Michael releases the big breath he's probably been holding since Bob collapsed.

'This shouldn't happen. The pilots have regular physicals.' Relief starts Michael talking, then Gregor, who's eased out of his seat and is wedged into what was his minimal foot-space, tells him to take over the mouth-to-mouth while he counts and depresses Bob's chest.

The counting has a rhythmic cadence that makes me think something's happening. I can see the airfield up ahead and grab the radio. Gregor always calls in our ETA to the hospital on the emergency channel ten minutes before we land, and Bob's had no reason to change channels.

'This is Foxtrot Oscar Golf, Hillary Green speaking. Our pilot has had a heart attack. We're returning to Merriwee, and need an ambulance with a defibrillation unit standing by on the runway. ETA two-seventeen—that's two-seventeen, eight minutes away.'

I pause then add, 'Might be an idea to have the fire service there as well. I haven't flown for a while.'

Gregor glances at me and I see the little quirk of his lips, so I know he knows I did it to lighten the atmosphere of panic in the plane. Although it's true. I haven't flown a plane this size lately.

Or ever.

'Is he breathing by himself?' I ask, glancing anxiously at Bob's ashen face.

'No, but he will be by the time we hit the ground, I

promise you,' Gregor says, while Michael, between breaths, complains about his choice of words.

The atmosphere is like that of an operating Theatre, where everyone is totally focussed on his or her job yet all use levity to keep the tautness out of fingers and the panic out of minds that are responsible for the life of the patient on the table.

I can see the ambulance screaming in as we descend, and imagine I can hear its siren. Behind it comes the fire truck, and I know it will be manned by men called hastily from their day jobs, so they'll look like clerks and stockmen but will do whatever job is required of them.

I fly past the strip, coming in low, checking the windsock, thinking about how Bob did it earlier, then turn and let her almost stall, dropping swiftly until the wheels kiss the earth.

I thrust the engines into reverse to pull us up and Michael cheers, but Gregor is already opening the plane door as we slam to a halt, me clinging desperately to the controls. Then he's out, dodging away from the propellers, racing to the ambulance, then dragging the trolley, set up with the defib unit, behind him.

The ambulance men follow in his wake, anxious but no doubt realising Bob means more to us than he does to them.

Michael has kept on breathing for Bob. It's ten minutes since he collapsed. Statistically, if it's less than ten minutes from cardiac arrest to defibrillation, the patient has a reasonable prognosis, but the odds get shorter with every minute after that.

Strong hands grasp Bob's sturdy body and he's lifted out. Gregor has the defibrillation paddles out, greased and ready to go. Michael rips Bob's shirt open, men step back.

Gregor shocks him once—a second time. I'm holding my breath and praying and making deals with God.

Bob's body jolts, then one of the ambos gives a cheer. Time for intubation, for feeding oxygen into Bob's depleted system. Time now to call for a medical evacuation, because he's far from in the clear.

Eventually, the ambulancemen load the trolley into the back of their vehicle, Gregor climbs in behind it and they set off for the hospital. Anna will be waiting there, ready to test his blood, hook him up to machines, find out why his heart failed.

I look at Michael, who smiles at me.

'I doubt I'll ever be airsick again,' he says, newfound confidence shining in his face. 'After thinking we were doomed to fly around up there until we ran out of gas and crashed, you saved the day, Hilly Dilly.'

He grabs me in his arms and we waltz around, celebrating the sheer joy of being alive.

'You two flying that plane out of here or do you want a lift to town?' one of the firemen asks.

Michael turns expectantly to me.

'I'm not flying that plane anywhere,' I tell the fireman, then turn back to Michael. 'Not now, and not ever. I was talking nonsense—boasting—when I told Gregor I'd flown bigger planes than that. I did have my licence once, and I've been mucking around in planes since I was ten, but they were little mustering planes. I've never flown anything that size before.'

Michael faints, which causes yet another drama. I let the firemen revive him and hold him in recovery position. I've done my bit for Flying Obstetrician and Gynaecology Service personnel today.

A familiar vehicle approaches. Tom Fleming, heading

back into town after spaying some cattle, has received a call from Anna to swing by the airfield and pick us up.

'Can't stay away from the place, eh?' he says, as he walks across to greet us. 'What happened?'

I explain because Michael's still looking far from well.

'You brought the plane down?' Tom sounds too incredulous and I straighten up to my full five-five—I kicked off my sandals before climbing over the seat and they must still be in the plane.

'I have had a licence,' I tell him, 'even if I haven't had time recently to put in the flying hours to keep it up.'

'Well done,' he says, and guides me towards the car, and I'm pleased his hand, resting in the small of my back, hasn't the same effect Gregor's had. I've reached the letdown stage and, with knocking knees and a pounding pulse, feel in need of a little support.

Michael staggers along behind us, muttering to himself. I think he's over being over being airsick. In fact, I doubt, now he's coming to grips with what actually happened up there, if he'll ever get into a small plane again.

'How do we get you and the plane back to base?' Tom asks as we're driving to town.

I've been thinking about it, so can offer my suggestion.

'If there's a local pilot available, we could hire him to fly us back then pay for his transport back to Merriwee. Otherwise I suppose we'll have to hire a car and drive back. Gregor has a full surgical list lined up for tomorrow at Bilbarra so we actually have three days to get the plane back to base before we need it for Monday's flights.'

Behind me Michael groans, confirming my suspicions about his future attitude to flight. I'd like to tell him that now he's had one mid-air emergency, it's statistically unlikely he'll ever suffer any more trouble, but I don't think he'd listen right now.

We arrive at the hospital, and Tom accompanies us inside.

'They'll have him in the trauma room,' Tom says, 'and I doubt they need more bodies in there. How about a cuppa?'

I try to smile because, more than anything else, the offer of a cuppa symbolises the pull-together spirit of the outback. Which is why tears are leaking from my eyes when Gregor comes out of the trauma room.

'He's doing OK but it's still touch and go,' he says, handing me a handkerchief almost automatically.

Then he touches my arm, very gently, and adds, 'You did a great job out there, Blue.' And my eyes leak a bit more.

CHAPTER EIGHT

'ONE of the nurses here has a husband with a licence. He can't fly us back tonight, but can take us first thing in the morning,' GR says.

Funny how he was Gregor in the plane—in the emergency situation—but he's now back to GR in my head. Talk about distancing!

'Anna has offered to put us up for the night. I'll stay here until Bob's flown out. I've contacted Dave and he'll tell Bob's wife, and as soon as we know where he's going, I'll let them know.'

'Will he make it?' I know it's a stupid question but I have to ask. GR looks at me, then shakes his head.

'You know the statistics as well as I do, Blue,' he says. 'I can't offer you false reassurance, but at least you gave him a chance by getting us all back down to earth as quickly as you did.'

'You and Michael gave him a chance with the CPR,' I remind him, not wanting to get weepy *again*.

Fortunately, Tom appears with a tray of tea things.

'I'll run you back to the house when you're ready,' he says, setting down the tray and waving towards the comfortable chairs in the hospital foyer. 'I've booked us all in at the Cattlemen's Club for dinner,' he adds. 'I could have cooked for you but they do the best steak in the midwest.'

GR heads back to the trauma room and Michael and I drink our tea then troop after Tom.

'Lost your shoes, Cinderella?' Tom asks, as I leap and hop across the sharp stones in the hospital car park.

'Left them on the plane,' I explain. 'I suppose I should go back out and get them if we're going out to dinner tonight.'

Tom offers to drive us out but I've had a better idea.

'No, just drop me at your shopping centre. I was going to shop this afternoon in Bilbarra, but I'll see what Merriwee has to offer.'

I get a little nervous flutter in my stomach as I say these brave words, but I know I *have* to get some boots and trousers of some kind for work. And surely a shop in Merriwee won't offer the kind of temptation shops in the city offer.

I mean, it's not as if they're likely to have designer clothes!

'You'll go into a shop barefoot?' Michael asks, in such scandalised tones I have to laugh.

'Yes, but I'll come out shod,' I assure him, feeling in the pocket of my cargo pants to make sure I have my credit card.

Tom doesn't argue. He drives up the main street and stops outside a huge shop which I know, from experience of country towns, will sell everything from shoes to bras to handkerchiefs.

Not a bad idea, the handkerchiefs, considering the way my eyes are leaking. I'll buy some for myself and a pack of new ones for GR.

'I'll be back in an hour—that give you enough time?'

'Plenty,' I assure him, and I hit the shop. I'm about to explain about my shoe-less state to the woman behind the counter that's midway down the store, but it seems the outback grapevine's working well.

'Oh, you're one of the flying specialists, aren't you?'

she says, rushing forward to greet me. 'Did you lose your shoes in the crash?'

'We didn't actually crash,' I tell her, but my eyes are on the racks of clothing beyond her counter and my feet are drawn involuntarily towards them.

'You've got Bliss brand clothes,' I murmur, stunned to see my favourite designer represented out here.

'Yes, the girl who runs the company is a niece of a local family. So, of course, we like to do what we can to support her.'

Seeing Bliss has just opened shops in New York and London, I don't know how much support she needs, but the thought's still there and I smile at the woman as my fingers flick along the hangers.

By this time I'm worrying about other recent purchases. I know I told you I was careful with money—but that's because I have to be, as I'm extremely weak when it comes to clothing.

And chocolates.

Just how maxed out is my credit card?

'If you don't have money with you, we can send an account to the hospital,' the woman says. I must be becoming increasingly transparent if everyone in the outback can read my mind!

'I really need shoes,' I tell her. 'I'm a size six, and I'd like some boots but smart boots, not too practical-looking.'

I'm lifting hangers off the rack now, folding the selection over my arm, telling myself I'm not going to buy all this gear, just while away an hour trying things on. But Bliss has gone with the 'combat' fashion this season, and there are wonderful cargo pants with straps and buckles and pockets everywhere. Sexy vests to go with them, and divine shirts—all khaki and green and brown, which are colours a redhead can wear without having people flinch when they see her.

Tom's waiting outside when I emerge, laden with bags. I remembered the handkerchiefs and bought some new undies as well. Now I'm longing to have a shower and put on clean—as in new!—clothes.

Of course, I've bought most of the clothes for work—all the pants and vests and shirts. But Bliss also does the sexiest range of almost-nothing dresses. They're quite discreet in that they don't leave acres of flesh exposed, but they have a kind of cling to them that not only feels great but looks sensational, even if you're only five-five and not supermodel material.

Of course, I don't put the one I bought on for dinner at the Cattlemen's Club, but can't resist wearing a vivid blue T-shirt, with BLISS in sequins across it, and a blue-green skirt—knee-length, I'm not going to compete with Dustbin's legs—which has similar sequins scattered here and there.

Gran would—will?—be horrified. She still believes sequins, rhinestones, any and all glittery trim belong on eveningwear, and are certainly not for dinner in a country town. But there are so many glittering garments in that shop, someone must be wearing them!

And high-heeled blue sandals. I *did* buy boots, but they're definitely not for going out in—not tonight.

Tom's 'Wow' as I enter his kitchen some time later is appreciated. Anna's not back but I've snitched a bit of her moisturiser and used the lip-gloss I now carry in my pockets both on lips and a touch on my cheeks so I'm not deathly pale.

'Thanks!' I tell Tom, though it isn't his 'Wow' I want. Deep inside I know GR isn't really a 'wow' kind of person, but I'd like him to be impressed. A car pulls up outside, and Tom goes out to see who it is, reappearing with his arm around his wife, GR walking behind them.

It's not 'Wow' but his hesitation when he sees me is worth nearly as much. His eyes skim down my body and come to rest on my sandals before lifting again to my face. The little smile is quirking up one side of his mouth.

'Been shopping, Blue?' he asks.

'I did buy boots,' I tell him, defiant because his teasing is now causing me nearly as much internal strife as his touch does. 'How's Bob?'

Anna has slumped into a chair by the kitchen table and Tom is massaging her neck and shoulders almost absent-mindedly, but their closeness makes me feel both warm and envious.

'He was conscious before we sent him on, and able to talk.' Anna answers my question, while leaning her head back against Tom's wrists so he can get at the tense bits at the back of her neck. 'Providing he doesn't have another major incident before they get him into Coronary Care, he should be OK. But there must have been some significant blockage somewhere in his circulatory system for him to suffer such a severe attack.'

'Once they get him into Coronary Care, tests will determine what's happened,' GR adds, as if knowing I'm in need of more reassurance. 'And do something about preventing it happening again.'

Michael drifts in, showered but not shaven, and wearing what is obviously a borrowed shirt.

'Beer?' Tom offers, and Michael nods, though I've a feeling he probably needs something stronger—like a straight whisky!

'Greg?'

Tom's crossed to the fridge, handed Michael a can, and is now holding one aloft in GR's direction. I'm also looking in his direction, trying to fit the shortened 'Greg' to the man. Can't do it—he's a Gregor or a GR. Gregs are way too ordinary!

'Not just yet,' he says, then nods in my direction. 'I'm not saying I'll be able to compete with my colleague, but if I can borrow a towel, a razor and a clean shirt, I'll do my best.'

Tom takes him away, and Anna stands up and turns to smile at me.

'Wonderful things, men, aren't they?' she says. 'Get the beers for the boys sorted, but forget about the women. I can offer you a gin and tonic, white wine, beer, of course, and I think there's some rum and whisky somewhere but I'm not sure what goes with it.'

'I'd love a gin,' I tell her. It has, after all, been a big day, and she hasn't offered chocolate.

She fixes me a drink then points to the veranda.

'Why don't you and Michael go out there? It's much cooler and the chairs are comfortable. I'll have a quick shower and change then join you.'

We follow her advice and I sink gratefully into a squatter's chair—loose canvas slung between a frame in such a manner it's like a hammock you can sit in. Great chairs for relaxing in at the end of a busy day.

I'm happy to sit in silence, but Michael is still wound up. He asks questions about where I did my hospital training, and we play 'do you know' for a little while, then footsteps herald the arrival of someone else, and I don't have to turn my head to know it's GR.

He might not have new clothes, but with his hair still damp from the shower, and his skin shiny from a shave, he looks good enough to give any woman palpitations, so his effect on me is galvanic.

Maybe he's right. A quick and very discreet affair

might be the answer. We might be incompatible in bed, and that would be that. All the fizzing, zapping, tingling stuff he's generating would go away and we could be normal colleagues.

I take a sip of my bed—*drink*, not bed, get with it here—and try to stop my mind pursuing the alternative: the 'what if we're not incompatible in bed' scenario.

Tom and Anna appear and conversation drifts around my head. I feel so at home in the chair on a wide veranda I wonder if I miss Rosebud more than I'm willing to admit. Was it something to do with knowing it would pass to Uncle Joel and from him to my cousin Brendan that made me determined to turn my back on country life?

'Blue?'

GR touches me gently on the shoulder.

'We're going now,' he says quietly, and I realise the others are moving towards the steps.

'You didn't make a joke about me being lost in my head,' I tell him as I stand up, grateful for his hand because they're hell to get out of, these squatters' chairs, but regretting the need because any touch, no matter how impersonal, affects me.

'You looked so sad I knew it wasn't time for joking,' he says, dropping my hand but standing close.

The attraction we both admit to buzzes between us and I can feel my body tightening with desire, my mind ordering resistance.

'Come on,' he says. 'They're waiting.'

It's a wonderful evening of good food and relaxed conversation, and if you're wondering how we can laugh and joke with Bob fighting for his life in some city hospital, I have to tell you we need to do it. If you don't take the opportunities to relax when they come your way, you end up so uptight you're useless to both patients and yourself. So though Bob hovers in all our minds, and our hearts pray for him to be OK, we still have fun, so much so I begin to wish it didn't have to end.

That reality didn't have to intrude…

Reality strikes in the darkness with a hand on my shoulder and GR's voice in my ear.

'Come on, Blue, wake up. We've got to grab something to eat and be out at the airfield by dawn.'

I sit up, so groggy I can't remember where I am. I didn't have *that* much to drink last night. It's lack of sleep. Knowing GR was in a bed just through the wall in Tom's big house disturbed me so much I counted four thousand, seven hundred and fifty sheep before I started counting articles of woollen clothing I'd like to own.

'Are you awake?' GR's voice is harsh. Has he been trying to wake me for so long he's getting cranky?

But then he groans and his hand slides off my shoulder, down my chest, touching my breast.

'You've got no clothes on.' It's a husky, muttered whisper, barely audible, but the combination of touch and sound ignite me so I tremble as his fingers brush my nipple and I hear him groan again as he drags me into his arms and holds me tight against him, then drops his head to claim my lips.

The buzz is so strong it explodes in my head, and I forget I've probably got dragon breath and kiss him back with frenzied helpless pleasure, wanting this never to stop but knowing it must stop right now.

Must stop!

I push him away.

'I didn't come expecting to stay the night,' I tell him, though I've already decided—some time in the sleepless watches of the night—to swallow my pride and bring my handbag in future. I can carry clean underwear and a shirt to use as a nightdress. And what if we'd crashed and I didn't have any chocolate?

Not that I tell GR any of this.

He stands up, hesitates then walks away, and I get up, check he's shut the door behind him, turn on the light and start rummaging through my new belongings for something to put on.

Too much choice for a change, but I haven't time to be picky. I grab the first things I come across and dress, then head for the bathroom where I borrow a bit of toothpaste and use my finger to smear it across my teeth.

I'll put a toothbrush in my handbag, too.

Note to self—check out bigger handbags if there's a handbag store in Bilbarra.

Everyone's in the kitchen by the time I arrive, Anna making toast, Tom pouring coffee into mugs, Michael pacing anxiously—no doubt at the thought of getting back in the plane.

Gregor's sitting at the table, already sipping at a coffee, looking so relaxed I wonder if the man who was groaning in my bedroom only minutes ago was a figment of my imagination. Then I see the tendons standing out in his neck and the tic of a nerve near his left eye.

He's as tense as I am, and once again I have to think about having an affair with him. Surely, if we don't and we both go on like this, we'll crack into a million tiny pieces.

Poor Mum, I think, surprising myself as I've never thought of her as Mum. Just 'my mother'—distancing myself as I've tried to do with GR. Now, suddenly, I'm imagining I know exactly how she must have felt when the

Argentinian swooped into her life, and my heart aches for her.

Tom takes us to the airfield, introduces us to the man who's helping out by flying us back to Bilbarra, then departs. The trip is calm, and the pilot doesn't have a heart attack, and before we know it we're back at Bilbarra hospital in plenty of time to start the day's operating list.

I call in to see Gran first. I did phone her last night, to explain we were delayed. Not that she'd have been too worried, she's still engrossed with Charles!

'The stupid woman at the home help service says he has to go on a waiting list for help,' she tells me almost before I've put down my purchases. She sounds really cross then relents. 'I don't suppose it's her fault, but fancy there not being enough people here in town who want to make a bit of extra money and do something useful at the same time.'

She doesn't wait for me to offer a comment, but rushes on. 'So I'm going to have to move in with him. I know you'll understand.'

Understand my grandmother moving in with a man?

I know she's only doing it to help him out.

Or is she?

It's not nice to imagine one's grandmother having a sex life of any kind, but to think she might be having a better one than I'm currently enjoying is the absolute end!

I try to switch my mind off sex. I even make the right noises so Gran doesn't feel guilty about leaving me. Leaving me? We've barely seen each other.

Leaving me?

The question repeats itself but this time with strong undertones of utter panic. If Gran's not here it leaves me vulnerable to all the impulses I've been trying to ignore.

She was my fall-back plan. The reason it would be impossible to have that affair with GR!

Fortunately, the operating list is diverse and interesting enough to take my mind off everything but gynaecological matters—apart from the very slightest frisson of awareness that hovers in the air around my body purely because of the proximity of GR.

We start with a cervical conisation, where GR uses a laser to remove a cone-shaped—hence the name—segment of tissue from the patient's cervix.

'It was showing some dysplasia,' GR explains, 'which may or may not have been pre-cancerous. I'll send some tissue away for testing.'

He works so competently I wonder if I'll ever be able to emulate his skills, but I move in closer to do the suturing and know I'll improve, not only through working with him but because, I must feebly admit, I'll be wanting to impress him. Pathetic, isn't it?

'Next we've got a D and C following a spontaneous abortion and intermittent bleeding.'

We're scrubbing for the next patient, side by side at the basin, hands busy with the little nail brushes, foam dripping from our elbows.

'Was it a first pregnancy?' I ask, and he shakes his head.

'No, she has one child but has miscarried several times, both before that one and after. She was really hoping this time she'd carry to term, so she's upset. That's why I've opted for a general anaesthetic rather than local. She doesn't need to be aware of what we're doing to her.'

There is so much genuine empathy in his voice I want to hug him but, given the water now sloshing around and our almost sterile hands, it's not a good idea.

It's not a good idea for other reasons either, but I'm honestly not thinking of them at the moment.

Well, not much.

We're gloved and waiting when the patient comes in, Michael hovering anxiously at her head. He introduces Becky Martin to me, and Becky smiles weakly, then turns to GR.

'Will it ever happen?' she asks, probably already sleepy from the pre-med, which explains her weepy voice.

Like I can talk. I'm swallowing hard just listening to her.

'Of course it will,' GR assures her. 'But remember what we talked about. Give your body time to heal for at least six months before you try again. You know that's important.'

Becky nods and her eyes close. Michael explains what he's doing, attaching monitoring equipment to her body, oxygen to a mask he settles on her face. She already has a cannula taped to her left hand, and he injects in the anaesthetic he's chosen to use.

Nods to GR and we're away. It's not a pleasant job. GR has to be very careful he doesn't damage the lining of the uterus. Again he talks as he works, educating me about the patient, explaining how she reached the second trimester this time before miscarrying. We discuss textbook cases of spontaneous abortion, and possible solutions we might eventually be able to offer Becky. Again, we keep some tissue to send to the labs to ensure there was nothing amiss with the foetus, then another patient is wheeled away.

'The next's a laparoscopy—query ovarian cysts, Blue,' GR says, as we sit in the little anteroom and drink a cup of coffee. 'Want to do it?'

'Do I want to do it? Do cats like fish? Dogs bark? Birds fly?'

He grins at me.

'I've got the picture. Done one before?'

I shake my head then assure him I've seen hundreds, which might be a slight exaggeration but not a big enough lie to have lightning strike me dead.

He smiles as if he knows I'm exaggerating, and goes on to explain exactly what I'll be doing, from the tiny incision in the abdomen to inserting the hollow tube through which we can pass a light source and a number of instruments.

I don't kill the patient—in fact, I do well enough to garner praise from 'the boss' and finish the day on such a high I float back to GR's office and agree to do the paperwork following the operations without even a grimace by way of complaint.

'Thank you,' he says. 'I really appreciate it, because Charles was discharged yesterday and I haven't had a chance to see him. I've no idea how he's going to manage on his own, unless your grandmother has found home help for him.'

I'm about to tell him Gran's the home help then realise he'll find out soon enough.

And, no doubt, figure the rest of *that* particular equation!

The paperwork of operations involves writing up exactly what we did on the patients' hospital files, checking the written orders to the nursing staff for post-op monitoring and treatment, writing a note—usually a form letter—for the patient to take home, which details what they should expect following the operation, how to look after themselves and what symptoms should be immediately reported to the doctor.

Then, in case you thought a surgeon's life was all Theatre gowns and scalpels, we have to write a letter to the referring doctor, usually the local GP, explaining exactly what we've done, what we've found and advising that a copy of the lab reports will be sent to them.

By the time I've finished this, it's nearly nine, and as the day started in pre-dawn darkness I'm feeling tired. That's until GR appears as I leave the office, striding down the corridor from the direction of the wards.

'I've seen Charles and checked on all our admitted patients,' he tells me, 'so, if you're finished in there, we're all done.'

We don't talk about him walking me back to the old quarters, but he does and I'm comfortable with it. Or as comfortable as I can be with desire and excitement spreading liquid fire along my nerves.

'Shall I say goodnight here?' he asks, at the bottom of the steps, and as if there's been an inevitability in this situation right from the first touch of our fingers and clasp of our hands, I shake my head and he walks up the steps behind me.

I'm so strung out I'm shaking, so I appreciate him taking me in his arms and drawing me close, supporting me against his body. We stand like that for a few seconds, but it's not enough. It was never going to be enough.

We kiss, but this time it's not only our lips exploring, but our hands—fingertips trailing across skin, fingers digging into muscle. I want to know his body as well as I know my own. Tactile, silent exploration!

There's no urgency now as we make our way, two bodies moving as one, towards the nearest cell, though my fingers fumble as I strip off clothes—his, mine, mine, his—and I feel him falter as he helps the process. Then, naked, squeezed together on the narrow bed, we again explore, touching each other, raising the excitement stakes to a point where I know I'll explode if we don't take that final step soon.

'There is still time to say no,' he says, voice harsh with wanting, the first time either of us has spoken distinguishable words.

I shake my head, then know he has to hear it.

'I won't say no,' I tell him. 'Can't say no!'

For a fleeting instant I wonder what my mother whispered to the polo player, then GR—Gregor—lifts his body over mine and we move to accommodate each other, finding that perfect fit so beautifully designed by nature.

I am not going to invite you into that tiny bedroom, and tell you the intimate details but, believe me, it was like nothing I'd ever experienced before. Soft and sizzling, sweet and frantic, a pulsating mix of sensations too ever-changing and various for words to do it justice.

I had enough, I wanted more, my mind gave in to sensation and let my body lead it wherever it wanted to go. And I must say, with all due modesty, that GR seemed to enjoy it, too. This is afterwards I'm telling you this, and I'm in the kitchen, peering into the refrigerator, mentally thanking Gran for being fixated on a balanced diet.

I put cheese, grapes, little plums, some slices of ham and a few dinner rolls on a platter and carry it back to where—Hell! Now I'm really in a bind. Surely after such wonderful intimacy he should be Gregor but, damn it, he's still GR in my mind. Anyway, he is sitting propped against the pillows, the light from the veranda filtering in enough for me to see him in all his naked glory.

Well, half his naked glory. He has a sheet pulled up to his waist.

He reaches out, not for the platter but for my hand, and pulls me down to sit beside him on the edge of the bed.

'That was very special,' he says quietly, and he leans forward to kiss me on the cheek.

I immediately go into after-sex panic, heart a-thump as the inevitable thoughts race through my head.

That's it? Goodbye? Is that why he's thanking me? Because there'll be no more?

But as I move, needing to put the platter down before I drop it, I realise there'll definitely be more, at least tonight.

CHAPTER NINE

HAVING only had one previous boyfriend, namely Pete, I'm not sure if the ensuing relationship—what happened after that momentous night—is normal or not.

It's kind of like things were, in that with Pete neither of us talked much about 'the relationship' right up until he heard the bells and whistles, when he mentioned, as if in justification for his overly enthusiastic response to Claudia, that we weren't exactly besotted with each other.

'In fact,' he had the hide to add, 'we're really more like friends who go to bed together because it's easier than finding someone else to have sex with.'

I think I chided him about ending his sentence with a preposition to hide my pique, but in retrospect he was right.

So now it's hard to judge the situation I'm currently enjoying.

We certainly don't talk about what's happening, GR and I, but going to bed together because it's easier than finding someone else—that's way off beam. We go to bed together because we can't help ourselves. Getting through the day without touching—let alone ripping each other's clothes off—is such a strain, we all but fly back to the quarters from wherever we've been, just so we can hold each other.

I don't know how discreet we're being. GR parks outside the rear entrance to the hospital rather than right outside the old nurses' quarters. Does that count?

And he goes back to his place some time during the

night, because he's never still beside me when I wake, though that first Saturday it was a close-run thing. The sun was painting colour in the sky when we tore ourselves apart and kissed goodbye.

We talk about other things—at least, I do. GR's not exactly chatty at the best of times.

But don't get me wrong, it's not every night we're together. Last Monday—B (for bed)-day plus three—Gran rang. We hadn't gone out to GR's property on account of Charles, and I spent most of the weekend in bed—either with you know who or alone, catching up on sleep. Anyway, Gran phoned on the Monday to say would I have dinner with her the following night so she could introduce me to Charles?

She explained she had to get some things from the quarters so would pick me up, and we had a very pleasant evening, Charles being a charming old rogue and me not being backward in questioning him about GR's childhood and youth and family and ex-girlfriends.

I wasn't really that blatant but I did discover he hasn't been previously married and, as far as his uncle knows, has no out-of-wedlock children scattered around the countryside.

For someone like me, this is important!

So, we reach the next weekend, and Charles is keen for Gran to see the property. GR's on call for emergencies and as I wasn't called out last weekend, odds are he'll be called out. This, I reason, is why he seems reluctant to go out to the property.

It isn't, of course. I figure that out when we get there on Friday evening. It's because being out there with the couple who manage the place, plus his uncle and my grandmother, sharing a bed will be out of the question.

So we go riding early Saturday morning. I can't be a

hundred per cent certain he has sex on his mind when we set out, but when we eventually stop by a creek that spreads at this particular point to a wide, waterlily-bedecked pool, it's almost inevitable something will happen.

Once clothed again, we lie, my head resting on his shoulder, and look up through the fern-like leaves of a northern wattle at sky so blue it makes my eyes ache.

'You're a beautiful rider,' he says. 'Natural. Like some aboriginal stockmen I've seen who seem to mould their bodies to the animal beneath them so horse and rider are one.'

And suddenly, weakened by a simple compliment, I'm telling him about my heritage. About my mother who lived to ride and in the end left Rosebud for Sydney where she ended up training polo ponies, working with a team owned by a wealthy businessman.

'The team went to Argentina for an international competition and my mother went along as well, but didn't return with the team. The horses were to be sold over there and Gran assumed she stayed on to look after them. She had postcards from my mother, then a letter saying she was returning to Sydney. Then nothing.'

I'm pouring all this out, and GR's lying very still beside me. His fingers brush against my hair and for some reason that gets me going again.

'Gran contacted the man my mother had worked for, who hadn't heard from her since she'd left his employment in Argentina. He said there was a man, a polo player, but refused to say any more. Then Gran gets a phone call from a hospital to say my mother had died, but left a child. Me.'

I pause for a minute, then add, 'So it's no wonder I can ride.'

GR shifts, propping himself on one elbow, puts on his glasses then looks down at me.

He touches my cheek, a brush as gentle as a butterfly's kiss.

'No leaking eyes?'

His eyes are kind, his lips soft, so I have to smile.

'It's not something I ever cry about,' I tell him honestly. 'I feel sorrier for Gran, who had to go to Sydney and take charge of a newborn baby. And then live with how unhappy my mother must have been not to contact her family when she was in trouble. It was Gran who suffered, and Grandad. There were times I thought I'd have liked to know something of the man who fathered me—to know I had a family, if you know what I mean—but if he didn't care enough to find out what happened to my mother, why should I care about him?'

GR hugs me, which is nice because it's a warm, friendly, comforting kind of hug with nothing even vaguely sexual in it. Then we untie the horses and ride back to the homestead, and I start feeling embarrassed about pouring out my secrets to this man.

Fortunately, he's called out to a breech birth in progress at Amberton almost as soon as we get back to the homestead, and as I don't want to stay out on the property, especially as Charles and Gran seem to be holding hands a lot, I go back to town with him.

Back at the old quarters, I think about a late lunch, but decide I'm not hungry. I'd rather brood. You know how women's minds work. I go from mortification that I've told him all that ancient history to thinking about the hug—was it asexual because it was a goodbye hug? He'd talked about a quick affair and somehow I've been managing to ignore the adjective. Now it's flashing like a neon light in my head.

How quick is quick? We've had a week. Does longer than a week move out of 'quick' dimensions? Back when we were just talking sex, not actually enjoying it, I joked about how long after we finished he'd be asking Lydia Dustbin to marry him, but nothing has been mentioned since.

Is he still thinking of it? Still seeing her?

This, of course, is when I remember the previous Tuesday. Has Charles told Gran about Lydia? Is that why Gran asked me to dinner that particular night? Why I didn't see GR later that evening?

Are all women's minds so neurotic, or am I worse than most? By now, of course, I've got it firmly entrenched in my head that he's just using me, and though I've enjoyed the experience—yeah, like I 'enjoy' chocolate?—OK, so I've found it dazzling and rapturous and indescribably erotic and exciting and sensuous and satisfying—where was I?

I know. I'm saying it wasn't exactly a turn-off for me, but I still feel hard done by, persecuted even.

All of which leads to disaster when he returns, quite late this evening, from Amberton. You can probably picture the scene. Footsteps on the steps outside, a perfunctory tap on the door, then he's striding down the veranda to where I'm sitting with my eyes fixed on the television screen, though I couldn't for a thousand dollars tell you what is on.

'So, how's the world's sexiest redhead this evening?' he says, swooping his arms around both me and the chair and kissing my neck.

Sexiest! That's what he said. Not the most beautiful, or the cleverest, or the most wonderful. Just sexiest. That's all it is between us. Sex.

I know you think I knew that, and I did—or thought I

did—but don't all women, deep down, believe it's more than that? Or want to believe it's more than that?

'I've got a headache,' I tell him, and, would you believe, the man doesn't get it. I suppose it's a measure of his niceness that he takes it literally. He's all instant attention, offering cups of tea. Have I taken something for it? Did I eat lunch? Have I had dinner?

'Honestly, Blue, you're so casual about eating it's a wonder your health doesn't suffer more.'

As I say no to tea and, no, I haven't eaten but I'm not hungry, he's standing behind me, massaging my neck. And my head. And it's wonderful.

Right now it's better than sex because, although I don't really have a headache, it shows he cares, doesn't it?

Am I pathetic or what? I've spent most of the afternoon figuring out he was serious about it being a quick and discreet—very—affair, and deciding I should tell him a week is quick enough for me, then one neck massage and I'm gone.

His fingers dig into my scalp and I'm almost purring, then he bends and kisses me behind my right ear.

'Stay right there,' he whispers, and his footsteps sound as he walks back along the veranda.

Just because he's kind doesn't mean he loves you, I remind myself, but I can still feel the pressure of his fingers on my neck, and now I'm remembering the other pleasures those fingers have given me. I'm on the Pill, I won't get pregnant, so why should it be a quick affair?

'I know you said you weren't hungry,' he announces, returning some time later while I'm still tormenting myself with unanswerable questions. 'But you have to eat.'

He smiles wickedly and adds, 'Keep up your strength!'

I want to smile back, but once again, even in a joke, he's emphasising the sexual nature of our relationship.

'I bought the noodles and vegetables you enjoyed the other day. Two servings, as I'll have that as well. And rice. And they had special dim sims Mrs Li made herself so I got a few of those as well.'

He's pulling food containers out of the plastic bag as he explains, setting them on the table, then getting plates and forks. He serves me rice, and noodles, adds two dim sims to the side of the plate and sets it down in front of me.

I sniff hard, because he's being kind, and I love him, and he'll probably go away, if not now then soon, and if not soon then later.

The love thing comes as a bit of a shock. I've suspected it, of course, because of the little hitches in my heart from time to time, and the way his kindness gets past my defences. I'll have to think about this later, I realise as he serves his own meal then sits down to eat, telling me about the breech he delivered.

'I was sure it would end up as a Caesar but the little blighter finally turned and popped out with hardly any further trouble. The midwife had tried turning him a couple of times, but he was stubborn.'

'Maybe he needed a man's hands,' I say, and he smiles at me across the table.

'Maybe,' he agrees, his eyes twinkling behind his glasses.

My heart squeezes so tight it's like a hard, hurting lump in the centre of my chest. We've had this kind of conversation all week, the innuendos keeping both of us primed for love-making.

That's the kind of thing I'll miss, I realise, and sniff again.

'Maybe you're coming down with a cold,' he says, caring again, while I pray my eyes don't start leaking and totally give the game away.

We finish dinner—there are no leftovers so I must have been hungry—and he clears everything away, washes our plates and forks, then comes across to where I'm rooted to the chair.

He squats beside me.

'I'd offer to put you into your purple pyjamas and tuck you into bed, but we both know what would happen,' he says, trailing the backs of his fingers down my cheek. 'So I'm going to leave and I want you to go straight to bed. I'll have to go back out to the property tomorrow, but I'll call in when I get back to see how you are.'

He kisses my cheek, tousles my hair with a feather-light caress, then walks away.

I want to call him back, tell him I lied about the headache. I want to weep and wail and gnash my teeth that he's actually gone because I lied. But deep down I know I need this time out. I need to think things through and be one hundred per cent sure of where I go from here.

I'm willing to admit I'm so sexually attracted to the man—whether as a result of my mother's genes or not—I'd do almost anything to stay in a relationship with him. But love has raised a whole new issue. Love can, and in this case inevitably will, lead to heartache, and is the sexual satisfaction worth the pain?

Gran is a great believer in divine retribution and, although I'd never admit it to her, I have to wonder about it when I wake the next morning with a thumping head, a stuffy nose and a throat that's been sandpapered during the night.

'It's more than just a cold, it's flu,' GR announces, hours later. He has called in as promised mid-afternoon on Sunday to find me shivering in bed. Being a doctor and up in these matters, he headed back to the hospital for a thermometer and has now read it as if my running a temperature confirms his diagnosis.

'Or the plague. Or pneumonia,' I moan.

'Well, with any of those three I don't want you near pregnant women or post-op patients so you'll stay in bed. We'll manage without you for a few days. I'll get Phil to come over and take a proper look at you, get you started on antibiotics and arrange for someone to bring meals over from the hospital.'

He tells me all this then bends over and kisses me on the lips.

I protest about sharing germs with him, but all he does is smile and my heart soars at his niceness. While I'm sick, I tell myself, I won't think about him not loving me. I'll just enjoy whatever brings me happiness. I can, of course, do this, because it's like eating chocolates without thinking about the calories. Women are born with brains able to compartmentalise such things, and I've had plenty of practice.

'It's not the plague,' Phil, one of the residents at the hospital, tells me. It's Monday afternoon and he's got the lab tests back from the swab he took of my throat the previous afternoon. 'It's the flu and unfortunately it's the new strain that's got everyone edgy. No deaths so far in Australia but overseas—'

I interrupt at this stage to tell him I'd just as soon not know about mortality rates for a disease I happen to be suffering from right now. I also express my dissatisfaction with the supposedly clean country air I've been breathing.

'How could deadly flu germs get out here?' I demand, albeit croakily.

'You probably brought them with you,' he tells me. 'You'd been hanging around hospitals in Brisbane, and it's been quietly incubating since you got here.'

My throat's too sore to tell him I didn't 'hang around' hospitals in Brisbane but worked in one with women who were there to have babies, not die of flu.

I make do with a glare that grows fiercer when he follows up this conversation with the announcement that he's putting me in hospital.

'In isolation. I don't want you infecting half the town. It's a good thing they thought of an isolation room when they built the new hospital, isn't it?'

He's so cheery I want to throttle him with his own stethoscope, but I know if I sit up so I'm close enough to get my hands on it, I'll probably faint. In fact, I feel so bad that, though I refuse to be wheeled across to the hospital in a bed, I do agree to a wheelchair.

'I'll send a nurse and an orderly to help you. You stay in bed until they get here. Don't worry about your toilet things,' he tells me. 'Gregor said he'd get them later and bring them over.'

So much for discreet! Or would Phil assume that because I work for GR he'd know where I keep my toothbrush?

I'm in the passion-killer pyjamas, of course, but they're so sweaty, the gowned and masked nurse who puts me to bed in the isolation room removes them, gives me a sponge bath, then produces a silky, lace-trimmed black nightdress which she proceeds to slip over my head.

'That's not mine,' I tell her, and her eyes twinkle so I assume she's smiling behind her mask.

'I know,' she replies, 'but the hospital had a wealthy tourist who was hospitalised here last year and, although she was full of praise for the service and treatment she received, she was appalled at the collection of hospital gowns we give out to people who don't come prepared. She sent us two dozen, all gorgeous, but as people usually bring their own we don't often get a chance to use them.'

I'm sick, remember, so this probably seems more bewildering than it would if I was well, so I don't argue. I'm in isolation anyway, so no one will see me in a garment that would look more at home on an actress trailing up the red carpet on Oscar night.

Refreshed by the wash, and with the cool silk smooth against my skin, I drift off to sleep.

'Please, don't tell me you had that nightdress hidden away somewhere in your belongings when all I ever saw you in were the passion-killers.'

GR's sitting beside me when I open my eyes. He's masked and gowned but his eyes, though twinkly with the joke, look anxious.

'Or that you wore it for Pete but only wore the pyjamas for me,' he adds in a sterner tone.

'It's hospital issue,' I tell him, then remember something else. 'And I don't think I wore anything at all with you.'

I know he's smiling because his smile always makes my skin tingle. To distract myself I look towards the window. It's dark outside.

'I must have been asleep.'

'For more than twenty-four hours. Phil says the antibiotics could do that. Knock you out. But I think he'll be as pleased as I am to know you've finally woken up.'

'Like Sleeping Beauty,' I suggest, and smile at him. 'Only with short red hair and freckles. Sleeping Not-so-Beautiful, they'd have to call me. Though probably at the moment I'm more like Sleeping Downright Ugly.'

'I think you're beautiful,' GR says.

'No, you think I'm sexy—it's sexual attraction,' I remind him, and he looks a bit startled. Then Phil, apparently alerted by a nurse than I'm conscious, appears and GR says goodbye.

What with the mask, he couldn't have kissed me, so I really shouldn't be disappointed.

I close my eyes, and try to re-orientate myself. Pretend headache Saturday evening, real headache Sunday, into hospital Monday, sleep…

This is when I realise it's Tuesday and we all know what that means. But GR visited *me* and, what's more, he stayed until it must have been way past time for Lydia to be serving dinner. You see how much more kindly I feel towards her when GR's with me, not her! Didn't mention the dustbin, did I?

By Thursday Phil has decided I'm not going to be Bilbarra's first flu-death statistic and agrees I can go home—which means back to the old nurses' quarters. Gran, who phones me daily, is still acting home help for Charles but promises to come back and look after me.

I point out that this isn't turning into much of a holiday for her, but she won't listen. I decide I'm still too weak to argue, and that GR will have to work out the logistics of our relationship—with Gran back in the quarters—if it's survived flu and hospitalisation.

This is a reasonable question seeing as I'll be back in the passion-killers unless I steal at least one of the sexy, elegant nightdresses I've been wearing while incarcerated. I'm considering this—if I'm wearing one when I go home, they can't expect to get it back immediately, can they?—when the nurse appears with freshly laundered lilac pyjamas—yes, the ones with the huge purple hearts.

GR calls in that evening, talks to me, talks to Gran,

tells me to hurry up and get stronger as he's missing me at work.

I'm looking straight at him so know he means just that—no innuendo, no suggestion of missing anything more than my assistance.

By the time I return to work on Monday, I'm frustrated, confused and heartsick. It's over and I know it. It was a quick and hopefully very discreet affair, only now it's me worrying over the discreet part because I'd hate the whole hospital to know just how quickly he tired of me.

'Tired?' he asks, as he drives back from the airfield that evening. Michael was at a conference so I did the anaesthetic work while GR operated.

'A bit,' I admit, though tiredness is the least of the sensations and emotions running amok in my body.

'You'll have to be careful. Really look after yourself, Blue. You know the complications that can follow flu. Things like congestive heart disease.'

'Gee, thanks for reminding me,' I say, wondering if it's because he thinks I might become a permanent invalid that he's gone off me. Pathetic, isn't it? I'm desperate for a reason for things to be over other than he's tired of me.

He pulls up outside my 'home'—there are no lights on so I assume Gran's gone back to Charles's place. His wrist's still in plaster and he can't get help. Anyway, GR cuts the engine and turns to face me.

'I know you didn't plan on getting sick but sometimes things happen for the best,' he says, voice very serious so I know the 'this is it' conversation is about to happen.

He touches his finger to my temple and brushes at a bit of hair.

'It gave me time to think,' he adds, and though I want to yell at him to get on with it—to get it said—I also want to savour every minute of his company, even if it *is* the last time we sit like this.

Even if my heart is leaking blood through cracks that widen with every word he speaks.

'I know we haven't known each other very long, so it's unfair of me to ask you to make any kind of definite commitment…'

He's lost me! I frown at him, trying to make sense of what he's saying. There are phrases like 'maybe we should see where it goes' and sentences like, 'Even though I've waited, thinking that I'd know, I don't want to confuse strong sexual attraction with love.'

I can feel my frown deepen so much I'll have permanently etched furrows on my forehead. He was right—I *should* have been a dermatologist, then I could have done my own botox!

I know I'm only thinking frown lines to quell the panic bubbling inside me. GR's stopped talking and is looking expectantly at me. I must be still frowning, for he says, 'Is the idea so repugnant to you?'

'What idea?' I demand, needing it put into plain English.

He half smiles.

'The idea of our mutual attraction perhaps being more than simply physical.'

He touches my face again and runs his thumb across my lips.

'Seeing if it might actually be love. Seeing where things will lead.' Then he adds the clincher. 'Perhaps to marriage?'

My mind goes blank, then starts up again at a thousand revs a minute.

'But you wanted someone tall and dark and unemotional, and my eyes leak,' I remind him. 'And then there's the dustbin, and I don't know who my father is, and listening to your Uncle Charles I know your family is very proper and they mightn't like you marrying someone without a regular father. And anyway, you don't approve of women O and G specialists. I'd have to stop practising when I have babies and then there'll be a shortage.'

I'm not halfway through the list when he leans forward and interrupts in the worst—best?—possible way. He kisses me, so I kiss him back, and it's ages later, when we're squeezed into the narrow bed again and he's stroking his fingers across my belly, that he says, 'How did dustbins come into your list of reasons why you couldn't fall in love with me? Are they some kind of recurring theme in your life?'

'I didn't say I couldn't fall in love with you,' I tell him. 'Just couldn't marry you.'

The mention of marriage must divert him, because he leans over and kisses me gently on the lips.

'I haven't asked you yet,' he says, then he untangles himself, swearing quietly about the inconveniences of my accommodation—even without Gran here—and suggesting I move in with him.

'And let the whole town know what's going on?' I screech.

'Would that be so bad?'

He says it quietly, as if my reaction has bothered him, but I know it's just the narrow bed and having to get up and go home. I'm reasonably certain he hasn't thought this through.

And even if he has, I haven't. I mean, I love the man, I'm sure of it, but he's not sure, and if it turns out it isn't love for him, then what do I do? Move back in here and have people feel sorry for me?

'You think about it,' I tell him. 'About the consequences.'

He's dressed by now and sits down on the bed.

'You mean what people might say if you move out again?'

'Why me?' I demand.

'Because it's my house,' he says, and I can hear him smiling.

'But you might ask me to go, or I might have to go because I know it isn't working—because I turn out not to be the love you've been waiting for.'

This is not a cheery thought, but one of us has to face facts.

'We'll talk some more,' he says, kissing me goodnight, then standing up and walking quietly away.

I slide out of bed and pad barefoot across to the louvres so I can see him cross the car park to his car, and see his face as he opens the door and the inside light comes on.

He's a serious man, not much of a talker, a wonderful doctor and the man I love.

Heart scrunching in my chest, I think about what he's asked of me, and I realise that while I could have continued the affair just as an affair—could have enjoyed every sizzling minute of it because I believed that's all I'd ever have from Gregor—this new idea is something entirely different. This is putting my heart at risk in a way an affair would never do, because with an affair my heart—and mind and other bits of me as well—had to accept from the start that it would end.

That's the whole point of affairs—they're not total, forever-and-ever-type commitments.

I'm tired and know I should be in bed, but my mind's racing with conjecture—with pros and cons and hopes and fears.

It's the fears that win in the end. The biggest fear is that he won't find me lovable. Sexy, yes, mildly amusing—his lips quirk at my jokes—a good rider, but lovable's miles away from those things. The fear is not entirely Pete's fault. It might just have been coincidence that we knew each other for six years before we moved in together, then it was only six weeks later that Claudia made his bells ring.

And I can't help thinking of my mother. Going back through the dates on the postcards Gran kept, I've always known she must have been at least four months pregnant when she left Argentina. Did my father not want the child? Not care about her? Or, four months into the relationship, did he find her unlovable?

'I don't want to shift in with you,' I tell GR, climbing into the car beside him the next morning.

'That's OK,' he says, so easily I have to wonder if he isn't relieved.

By the time we're pulling up at the roadhouse I've stewed over it for so long I have to ask.

'Did you think about it and decide it wasn't a good idea? Is that why you're not arguing?'

He turns towards me. I'm sure it must be the glasses that make him do surprised so well.

'Why should I argue? It's your decision and I respect that.'

'So we can keep seeing each other?'

Little smile!

'We can hardly help it, can we? We work together.'

CHAPTER TEN

IT's TUESDAY, so we're back in Amberton to see Mel. This time a tall, blond man is with her, introduced as Angus, still in shock at the thought he's going to become a father of four.

'She's saying she wants to have them in Bilbarra but she'd be better off in Brisbane, wouldn't she?' he asks GR, before we're even in the consulting room. Mel was booked as first patient so we could both see her before GR starts operating.

'Yes.' GR agrees with the anxious father-to-be. 'Not because we couldn't handle the multiple birth but because we might not be available if something happened and you needed help urgently, Mel,' he adds, holding her hand and looking down into her flushed face.

'Down in the city there's always someone available, and the very best neonatal care. And you should go down there soon—like next week. You know your blood pressure is up. You need more constant monitoring than we can give you.'

'We can go today,' Angus says, then as Melanie starts to argue, he quells her with a frown. 'Of course we can. We'll fly on down from here. You don't fit into any of your clothes so you can buy a whole new wardrobe.'

Surely music to any woman's ears, but Melanie is still looking fretful.

'But you won't be there,' she says, and he leans down and kisses her. 'You bet I will,' he promises. 'If that mob back at home can't run the property without me for a few months, then that's too bad. I'm coming with you and I'm staying with you,' he says, taking hold of the hand GR had been holding and looking very masterful. 'We'll get through this together.'

Of course, Melanie starts to cry and GR looks immediately at me, so I blink a few times and swallow hard and smile to assure him I'm not being overcome with maudlin sympathy.

GR suggests a specialist friend of his who'll take Melanie as a patient, and goes off to phone him. Angus goes as well, to ring various agents he has in the city and organise accommodation close to the hospital.

I stay behind to do doctor things, like taking blood pressure, testing urine, talking to Mel about how she feels.

'Terrified,' she admits. 'It's far worse, knowing all the things that can go wrong. I'm also a bit worried about Angus. He's going to drive me nuts, fussing over me for the next twenty weeks.'

'You won't go full term,' I remind her, 'so it won't be quite that long.'

'Well, thank you, but as I can't imagine Angus with nothing to do for a couple of days, even two weeks with me as his sole project is terrifying.'

'Get him a computer and let him do the business work of the property from Brisbane,' I suggest, knowing that worked when Joel broke his back in a motorbike accident and had to stay in Brisbane for months for therapy.

'Brilliant idea. I might also be able to get him involved in something at the hospital. I can't see him as a visitor, but maybe there's a charity of some kind that could use a man with too much time on his hands on a temporary basis.'

'And you'll have to shop. Or he will. You might not

feel like doing the rounds of the baby stores, but someone will have to.'

Melanie looks up at me.

'Do you think so? Do you think I'll be able to carry them? Keep them all?'

'I'm sure you will,' I tell her, and for some reason I'm confident I'm right.

Dave flies us home. We talk about Bob, who is still in the coronary care unit in Brisbane because he's had a triple bypass by now and is recovering from that.

'Jake will take you tomorrow. He's flown for the flying surgeon and knows the towns you'll visit. It's Turalla tomorrow, isn't it?'

GR confirms this and I wonder how many more towns I've yet to visit. We do fortnightly trips to some places, monthly to others, and from what I remember of the schedule, some are visited every six weeks.

He's talking to Dave so I can see most of his face, and I'm thinking of weeks—of twenty-one weeks, in fact—the twenty-one weeks left in my twenty-four week contract out here.

Will I be moving on?

I take a great gulp of air to stop the panic I can feel just thinking about not being with or near GR.

Gregor...

Can I use his name?

Is it safe?

I'm still lost you know where when we touch down. GR's mobile rings and he pulls it out, talks to someone, frowns, then suggests that Michael drives me home. Nothing else, no explanation, no 'see you later'.

But he's frowning, and I realise it's Tuesday and I can't

help wondering if it was Lydia who phoned and if that's where he's going.

He's an honourable man, my head tells me. Too honourable to be seeing Lydia while he's having an affair with me. But this rational information doesn't stop my heart behaving as if it's been severed from its ties.

Michael drops me back at the quarters, and Gran's there.

'I thought you'd moved back in with Charles,' I tell her. 'I'm OK now. I can look after myself.'

She sits down at the table and I realise she's pale—not like herself at all.

'Gran, you're not sick? Don't tell me I've given you the flu.'

'No, love,' she says, 'but something's happened. There's something I have to tell you. Come and sit down.'

'Uncle Joel? Jill?'

'No, it's not bad,' Gran assures me. 'Just unexpected.' She's frowning as I sit down opposite her.

'Very, very unexpected.'

'You're going to marry Charles,' I guess, glad it's not something bad but puzzled as to what could have sent her into a spin.

She shakes her head.

'Are you going to tell me?' I demand. 'Or do I have to keep on guessing?'

'It's your father,' she whispers, reaching out to take my hands and hold them tight. 'Apparently he came to Australia, looking for your mother, and flew up to Rosebud, which was the only address of your mother's he ever knew, and saw Joel.'

My heart's racing, I've definitely got palpitations, my hands are sweating and I realise I'm angry. No, I'm more than angry, I'm furious.

'After twenty-eight years he's come looking for my mother?' I yell. 'What a hide! How dare he? Did Joel tell him to get lost? To stay away? To drop dead?'

Contrary, isn't it? I really have, deep down, always wanted to know at least something about my father, and now he's in the same country I want nothing to do with him.

'Joel told him about you. He didn't know Nell was pregnant when she left. He'd been upcountry and got back to the city where the stables were—where she was living—to find she'd gone.'

'It was still twenty-eight years ago,' I remind Gran, who seems as if she's willing to forgive this man.

'He was married,' Gran says. 'In a country, and with a religion, where marriage vows are taken seriously.'

'But not seriously enough for him not to cheat on his wife—to have an affair with my mother.'

Gran doesn't answer. She looks at me for a moment, then shakes her head.

'Joel told him about you, Hillary,' she says quietly. 'He's on his way here, to meet you. Gregor's waiting out at the airport to meet him and bring him into town.'

'Gregor's waiting there? How did he come into this?'

'I asked him,' Gran says. 'I kept phoning until he touched down and turned on his mobile. I explained I'd have to talk to you but that you'd probably be upset. He wanted to do whatever he could to help.'

I close my eyes. I'm confused enough about having a love affair, now I have to handle having a father as well.

'I'm still getting over flu,' I remind Gran. 'I think I'll go to bed.'

Gran just looks at me as if she has no idea how to help me. Which she probably hasn't. I've no idea how to help myself!

A car pulls up outside before I've time to get my knees sufficiently under control to put the going-to-bed plan into action.

'They're here!' I'm panicking in earnest now and not a chocolate nibbly in sight. 'I don't want to see him, Gran. I'm not ready for this. I don't need a father now.'

Then GR's striding down the veranda. Alone.

'Need chocolate?' he asks, smiling so sympathetically I want to burst into tears.

'I don't need a father,' I tell him.

'Perhaps not, but think about whether you'd like to meet him as a person who, I think, from what he's told me, genuinely loved your mother. Your grandmother probably told you he was married. What he didn't tell Joel was that his wife was an invalid, injured in a riding accident and confined to a wheelchair. He couldn't bring himself to leave her, and your mother—and you—suffered as a result.'

He drops into a chair beside me and takes my hand.

'You show compassion to your patients, Blue. Couldn't you spare just a little for this man?'

He reaches out and takes my chin, tilting my head so he can look into my eyes.

'Didn't you tell me you'd like to know about your father? About your family? Wasn't it one of the reasons you told me I shouldn't consider marrying you—that you didn't have a proper father?'

Gran's probably having conniptions by now—seeing Gregor touching me, hearing marriage talk—but I'm mesmerised by the way his eyes are challenging me so I can't check on Gran's reaction.

'He's very proper,' Gregor adds. 'I've dropped him at the Buckjumper Motel and told him I'd phone after I'd talked to you.'

'To tell him what?'

I'm confused, angry, terrified—I can barely make my lips work to form the words.

'To tell him your grandmother and I have talked to you, and that you're thinking about things. Or I could tell him that all three of us will join him there for dinner tomorrow night. We wouldn't let you go through this on your own.'

Boy, is it ever hard to stop eyes leaking when this kind of conversation is happening.

I take a deep breath, blow it out, then nod.

'I guess if I've got to meet him then it's best to get it over with. But if we make it tomorrow night, I won't sleep tonight and I'll be useless tomorrow.'

Then I look at Gran and see how tired she looks and realise this is just as momentous for her as it is for me. How has she felt all these years? Has she thought of this man as responsible for the death of her daughter? Has she harboured bad feelings against him?

I can't imagine Gran harbouring bad feelings about anyone, but I've never lost a daughter.

I put a hand on her arm.

'Maybe we should leave it until tomorrow,' I say to Gregor, then I turn to Gran. 'Is that all right with you?'

Gran nods.

'I think it's better if we have a bit of time to get used to the idea,' she says, colour seeping back into her face.

Gregor nods, then stands up.

'I'll be going,' he says. 'I think you two women have had enough excitement for one night.' He bends down to kiss me on the cheek, says goodnight and pulls out his mobile as he walks away from us.

Then he turns.

'I'll pick you up in the morning, Blue,' he reminds me,

and the smile that accompanies the words reminds me of so much more I want to beg him not to go.

But Gran's upset, so it's my turn to tend to her, and I need to get my head around having a father before I start work tomorrow. I don't want to be upsetting sick or pregnant women in Turalla.

I fix some dinner for us both, and we talk, not much but saying things we've never said to each other before. Me, how much I love her, and how much I appreciate the wonderfully happy childhood she and Grandad provided for me.

She, how much I mean to her and how proud she is of me.

'And Gregor?' she asks, when we've done the dishes and are sitting in the lounge chairs looking at a blank TV screen. 'What about him?'

'I don't know, Gran,' I tell her, answering as honestly as I can. 'I love him, I know that much. He's attracted to me, but whether it's love on his side is a whole different matter. He wants to explore it, but I'm afraid if we do, and he finds it isn't what he's looking for—'

'That you'll be hurt.'

Gran finishes the sentence for me but offers no advice. We both know there isn't any to offer.

Turalla's different. Oh, it's got huge grain silos and a railway line, but from the air the first thing you see is the massive, open-cut coal mine just out of town. You see these going out from Bilbarra, too, but nowhere near this size.

A wardsman meets us in the Health Department car and drives us to the hospital. It's yet to be remodelled as most of the places we visit have been, and is an old timber building with wide verandas all around it.

A man in a crisp white shirt and tailored shorts comes out to greet us.

'Hi, Gregor, Michael,' he says, then puts out his hand towards me. 'I'm Mike Nelson, Director of Nursing. Welcome to Turalla.'

Gregor, who's said very little but has stayed deliberately close to me, even putting Michael into the front seat in the plane, introduces me.

'Nice to see a woman back in the job,' Mike says. 'For a while there I thought Gregor had frightened them all away.'

The man's so nice I smile at him.

'He tried to frighten me but it didn't take,' I tell him, as he leads us into the hospital.

Turalla is our only stop, because of the distance from Bilbarra and also because we only come here every six weeks. There's a full list of patients to see and GR has a big day ahead of him in Theatre, so he won't be able to help out if I get behind.

This, I tell myself, is a very good thing as I'll have no time at all to think about what lies ahead of me this evening.

As if I can *not* think about it. There's a bit of my brain chewing away at it the whole time, like a dog with a rag toy.

I'm shown into a spacious room. New hospitals are nice, but some of them tend to be a little cramped. This is great. I'm looking admiringly around, acknowledging an introduction to Anne Jackson, who'll be the nurse assisting me, when this gorgeous blonde zooms in.

'Hi, I'm Caitlin and I wanted to catch you before you started to say Connor and I want you to have lunch with us. Don't say no, I won't listen.'

Then she's gone again.

I look at Anne—dark-haired and attractive, with a glow about her as if good things are happening in her life.

'That's Caitlin. She and our local GP, Connor Clarke, are getting married next week. She's also a doctor, but she does research.'

In Turalla? I think, but part of me is also acknowledging how adaptable medicine is as a career. Maybe GR is wrong about O and G for women—surely there'd always be something we could do!

My first patient is Mrs Robinson. She's in her eighties, and has just discovered a lump in her right breast.

'I'll need to speak to Dr Prentice about this,' I tell her. 'The problem is, I can use a needle to take a little sample of the tissue in the lump, but even though we'll have the results back in a few days we won't be back here for another six weeks to talk to you about it.'

'I'm going to Brisbane to stay with my daughter next week,' she tells me. 'I could go to her doctor down there.'

'Can you stay down there if they want to operate?'

She nods.

'My daughter wants me to stay down there for ever, but I'd miss my friends and the things I do here. I work at the craft gallery on Tuesdays, and on Thursdays I read to the old people at the nursing home, and on Sundays I teach Sunday school…'

I'm still wondering how old the 'old' people she reads to are, while she continues the list.

'Well, seeing your daughter's doctor while you're down there is probably an excellent idea,' I tell her, when the recital of good works finishes. 'You can sort everything out while you're in the city and come back ready to go again.'

I don't give her a referral, because her daughter may already have an O and G specialist she will want her mother to see, but I write a note for her to take with her and wish her well.

I work through the morning, and am about to stop for lunch—GR having put his head in the door to see if I'm ready—when Anne comes in, looking worried.

'It's Betty Russell. The Russells are a big family in town, and though she hasn't got an appointment she's just seen Connor at the surgery and he's sent her straight across. Prolapse.'

Once again, the six-week gap between visits seems way too long.

'Send her in then find Gregor. He'll have to try to fit her in this afternoon. She can't wait six weeks for attention.'

I examine Betty, and Gregor appears as I'm explaining to her what has happened and that the situation is so severe only an operation will fix it.

'That's OK,' Betty says cheerfully. 'I've had my kids and my husband's gone off sex so I don't have much use for that bit of my body anyway.'

'We don't actually sew it up,' I tell her. 'If your husband gets interested again, it'll be the same as before. It's further inside you, the bit we'll take out.'

GR grins at me and the excitement I can't totally control when we're together blots out, for an instant, the worry about my father.

He takes over the explanation, getting oral permission for the operation, while I go off to get forms for written consent and to alert Michael to the fact we're squeezing in another op.

GR's discussing possible reasons for Mr Russell going off sex when I return, and Mrs Russell's looking quite excited about getting him checked out by the local doctor.

'I do miss it,' she confides to GR, who smiles, then winks at me.

'As you would,' he says calmly.

Michael's been summoned, and he and Mike take Betty through to the theatre anteroom.

GR turns to me.

'You'll assist?'

I nod, unable to speak as I look at this man who, in such a short time, has come to mean so much to me.

He *must* be able to read my mind because he leans forward and kisses me very gently on my lips.

Then it's back to business and, instead of having lunch with the beautiful Caitlin, we perform a hysterectomy on Mrs Russell. Then, once again, GR and I find ourselves in a changing room together, flinging Theatre gear off and fielding the inevitable currents of excitement that nothing seems to dispel.

'Are you OK? Did you sleep?'

I realise he hasn't mentioned the drama of my father in front of Michael or Dave.

In case I change my mind about acknowledging him? Or because he's naturally discreet?

'I'm OK and I slept,' I tell him, which is nowhere near the truth, and as I realise that I add, in a very small voice, 'But I could do with a hug.'

He folds his arms around me and holds me close. It's as asexual an embrace as we have ever shared but it works wonders, allowing me to straighten up and think ahead to the afternoon's work.

Caitlin and her doctor fiancé, Connor, are waiting for us in the consulting room.

'You couldn't come to us so we brought sandwiches to you,' Caitlin explains, introducing Connor and glowing at him with that peculiar radiance of love. 'Mike's taking some to Michael and he'll watch Mrs Russell while Michael eats.'

GR's explaining to Connor what we've done and I'm watching him—GR, that is—instead of listening to Caitlin.

Then she stops talking and I turn to her and see her smile.

'I haven't known him very long but he seems a lovely man,' she says softly, and I realise I must have been mooning or in some other way betraying how I feel.

'Don't worry about it,' she adds in a husky whisper. 'I think when you're newly in love, like me, you're sensitised to love in other people. Look at the shine in Anne's eyes when you see her later. An unhappy love affair looks as if it's finally coming right for her.'

I nod to Caitlin, acknowledging her prescience, but don't mention the larger problem that's just arrived in my life.

The Argentinian.

We finally head for home. It's late and I'm exhausted, so heaven knows how GR must feel after operating all day.

'We can put off tonight's dinner,' he tells me, tucking me into his car with unusual solicitude for the drive back to the quarters.

'And have another sleepless night worrying about meeting him?' I demand. 'No way. This is something both Gran and I need to get done.'

He starts the car and speaks without looking at me.

'Would you rather I wasn't there?'

Jeepers—what's that mean? He doesn't want to be there?

The thought panics me so much I blurt out, 'You don't

have to be there if you don't want, but I thought—I mean, you said—'

He reaches out and takes my hand, still looking at the road.

'I'd like to be there for you,' he says quietly. 'I would like that in whatever capacity you might consider me. As your boss, your colleague, your friend or your lover, Blue. Any or all of those things.'

'You'll make my eyes leak if you say things like that,' I tell him crossly. 'And I'll have to meet my father with red eyes and blotchy skin. It's the curse of the redhead.'

He grins.

'I think he'll understand that part at least,' he says, and I stare at him.

'He's got red hair? My father's got red hair?'

'Well, it's more grey than red now, but you can tell it was red,' GR says, now sufficiently diverted to glance towards me. 'Does that matter?'

I don't know why, but it does. But I can't explain so I just nod.

Naturally, by the time we make it to the motel I'm a nervous wreck. I've told GR we'll meet him there, and his appreciative whistle when I turn up in the shimmery blue Bliss dress I bought in Creamunna raises my confidence a couple of notches. Which brings it from about subterranean level to almost ground level.

Alex Costas is a grey-haired man of medium height. GR introduces us, Alex takes my hand, and both our eyes leak. I'm glad GR's there because after what seems like about five hours of this hand-holding, eyes-leaking stuff I still can't find my voice, and GR kind of pulls us apart, introduces Gran then steers us all into the dining room where he—I assume it was he—has arranged a private alcove for us. Not that anyone else is dining in the

Buckjumper's dining room this late at night. Country people tend to eat earlier than nine-thirty.

GR also steers the conversation ably, asking Alex how long he will be in Australia, what parts he's seen, what his first impressions are.

We order meals and drinks—GR handles most of this as well but I must have indicated some preference as I find I'm sipping white wine.

Alex recovers far more quickly than I do. He makes all the right noises in response to GR's questions—he flew into Sydney, stayed there some days, enquiring about my mother, loved the harbour and liked the friendly people. He then explains that he can only be away a month on this visit as important business guests are flying in from Europe to stay with him.

He turns to me and takes my hand in his.

'I would very much like you to accompany me back to Argentina, so I can introduce my daughter to her family.' He pauses, and I know my eyes are going to leak again because his are moist already with whatever he's going to say.

'You are my only child, and although, through not knowing of you, and to my eternal shame, I have done nothing for you these past long years, eventually you will, naturally, be my heir. In the meantime, I would beg you give me time to get to know you better—and for you to learn to know me.'

GR hands me a handkerchief, but I'm too shocked to need it. I can't believe I haven't, at any stage in the past twenty-four hours, given thought to what might happen after this meeting. You might not believe anyone could be so dumb but, honestly, it never occurred to me to think past tonight.

Alex is talking to Gran, including her in his invitation

to visit Argentina, telling her he has much to make up to her for what happened to her daughter. Then he gets angry.

'I cannot believe she didn't tell me. That she just took herself away, leaving me a letter saying she no longer loved me. I could not make my heart believe it. I was her first—her only lover. I adored her and she, I thought, felt the same way about me, then, poof, she's gone, leaving me just that silly note.'

'But you couldn't have married her,' Gran reminds him, and he shakes his head.

'No, you are right, and what I did was wrong, loving her as I did, accepting love from her. But I promise you, I would have cared for her and for Hillary. They would never have wanted for anything.'

Gran nods but I know she isn't completely satisfied. Then, as the meals are delivered to the table, Alex blows us all away.

'Did you name her Hillary? Choose her name?' he asks, turning to Gran, who shakes her head.

'Nell left a note. It said, "I'm sorry Mum. If it's a girl, would you call her Hillary?" She spelt it that way, with two "l"s, which is unusual.'

'It is my second name,' Alex says. 'After my mother, who was English.'

I push away my meal and stand up.

'I'm sorry, Alex. I can't stay here right now. I need to get away and think. I'm sorry, and I'll see you again. We'll talk some other time, but I can't talk, or eat, or even breathe properly right now.'

GR stands with me, glances at Gran to check she's OK on her own, then walks around the table, puts his arm around my shoulders and steadies me as we leave the dining room.

'I'm named after a grandmother I didn't know I had? I can't handle this, Gregor.'

He gives my shoulders a squeeze, then drops a kiss on the top of my head.

'I think that's the first time you've ever called me Gregor,' he says, his smile warming the words.

I turn towards him and offer the best I can in the way of a smile of my own. 'I suppose now I need to keep all the distance stuff for Alex,' I admit, and he hugs me again.

'I'm taking you home to my place,' he says. 'Tonight's not a good night for you to be on your own—not when you're in shock.'

'What about Gran?' I ask. 'She's in just as much shock as I am.'

'Then she'll probably go to Charles's place, not back to the old nurses' quarters anyway.'

I decide I'm too confused to worry about Gran and drop the subject. Besides, I've never been to Gregor's place, and the way he's talking, we're about to get to spend the whole night together. He might even have a decent-sized bed.

He does, and we use it to advantage, but with a slow and gentle love-making that warms every cell in my body and makes me, for an hour at least, forget I have a father.

Then Gregor props himself on his side and runs his fingers through my hair.

'You should go back with him,' he says quietly, but the effect of the words is like a pistol shot and I shoot up in the bed and glare at him.

'What? What are you saying? Do you want me to go so you can say "I told you so" about women O and G specialists? Is that it, or is an easy way out of this affair for you—so you'll be free to propose to the dustbin?'

I'm ranting and I know it, but we've just made wonderful, beautiful, magnificent love and he's telling me to go to Argentina. I carry on ranting, and rave a little as well, and he lets me, waiting until I run out of steam to remind me, very calmly, that it's what I've always wanted—to find my father, meet some family.

'You told me that,' he reminds me, which makes me angrier, so I clamber out of bed, gathering my clothes, scrambling in the darkness of this unfamiliar room.

'Stop that,' GR orders, but I'm beyond calming, pulling on the dress, cursing its slinky lines which make it difficult to drag on quickly, searching for my sandals, finding one, and my undies, and my handbag…

He stops trying to stop me and dresses himself. I hear the clunk as he picks up his car keys. He drives me home, silent and brooding—well, he's silent, I'm brooding and occasionally giving off huffs of anger. I can understand why dragons breathe fire.

'Do you want some time off to spend with your father?' he asks as we pull up outside the old quarters.

'No, he's here for a while, I can see him in the evenings.'

I open the car door and climb out, and he meets me halfway around the bonnet.

'Blue?'

He says it softly, and the silly nickname makes my heart skitter with delight, but I brush past him, clomping up the steps and into the old building.

He doesn't follow, and I'm left with my own thoughts for company. Gran, as GR supposed, is not home.

CHAPTER ELEVEN

GR ARRIVES the following morning and it's as if nothing ever happened—and I mean *nothing*! He's as cool and noncommittal as he was the first week I was working with him, talking about patients and operations and plans for the day and week.

And it's killing me.

It's not that we've been kissing and canoodling all the way to work recently, but there was a warmth in the car, and a teasing kind of tension as if a lot of lovely secrets lay between us, like parcels waiting to be unwrapped.

This morning the air is cool enough for me to grow icicles on my ears. I tell myself this is good—that a break-up was inevitable and at least with Alex here I'll have other things to worry about apart from heartbreak.

But GR's been kind and I behaved badly last night, so as we pull up at the roadhouse I reach out and touch his arm.

'I'm sorry if I said things that upset you last night. I was a bit overwrought.'

'Just a bit,' he teases, the ice melting in an instant. He covers my hand with his. 'You've a tough time ahead, Blue,' he adds, turning so he can look into my eyes. 'And a heap of emotional stuff to sort out with Alex. What worries me most is that I might have inadvertently made that hard for you, saying things about women O and G specialists, which were purely personal opinions. Going back to Argentina with your father makes sense. It's not for ever—you can slot back into the O and G programme when you get return.'

He sighs, then adds, 'The trouble is, Blue, you're so darned stubborn you'd turn down an opportunity like that just to prove me wrong.'

I feel like biting him, but make do with words instead.

'I might be stubborn, but you're so darned stupid you can't see that I'm in love with you! That I turned down the opportunity not because of a stupid job but because I didn't want to be parted from you! I know you don't feel the same way and that it's too soon, and not the way love should happen but, there, now you know.'

I get out of the car and almost slam the buckling metal but remember just in time. I stride into the roadhouse— I'd have stalked, only you need high heels for a really good stalk and I'm back in elastic-sided boots—and order bacon, eggs, tomatoes and hot chocolate for breakfast.

Michael, who's already at a table, looks nauseous. Unfortunately the plane incident hasn't helped his motion sickness at all.

'You've got to be joking!' he says. 'Hot chocolate with all that grease.'

'Grease is good,' I tell him, as GR joins us in time to give the waitress his order.

But he doesn't comment on my breakfast when it arrives, and we eat in silence, Michael sipping at his coffee and making occasional comments about the other early morning customers.

I try to read GR's face. In fact, for the rest of the day, whenever we're together, I attempt that impossible task. He's back to bland—no emotion whatsoever, so if he's horrified by my impassioned declaration of love, he's not showing it.

*   *   *

I spend the day in limbo—love declared but not acknowledged. GR has to go out to his property from the airport so Michael drives me back to the nurses' quarters. I borrow Gran's car and visit Alex that night. He seems a nice man, and more and more I come to realise that he genuinely loved my mother.

And more and more I have to think what I'd have done under the same circumstances. Loving GR as I do, I can put myself in my mother's place. So would I have left, knowing I was pregnant with a child who could cause problems in my loved one's life?

I can't answer that, but feel closer to my mother than I ever have before.

'Now I know about you, I am sure she said what she did—about not loving me—to protect me,' Alex says as we sit over coffee in the dining room. 'Love is such a strong emotion, it confuses us at times.'

'You can say that again,' I tell him, and he looks a little confused. Spanish is his first language so some of our clichés might not translate.

'You are saying you're confused? About Gregor?'

I nod, and suddenly I'm having a father-daughter conversation with a father I hadn't known I had, pouring out my heart to a man I barely know.

'I am going there this weekend,' Alex says, when I finish my tale of woe. 'You will also be at his ranch?'

This is news to me, though GR did say something yesterday about showing Alex his cattle.

Gran's back at the quarters when I return, and she knows about this as well. Apparently we're all to go out there—Alex, Charles, Gran, me—all playing happy families.

*   *   *

'It would have been nice if someone had asked me,' I grouch at GR when we meet for lunch after the morning consultations in his Bilbarra rooms.

'I did and you said yes,' GR tells me, 'but as you've been inhabiting a world of your own the last few days, it probably didn't sink in.'

'Well, I don't want to go.' I'm still grouching, and sulking, too, most probably. Wouldn't anyone who'd declared their love on Thursday morning—very early!—if by Friday lunchtime the recipient of the declaration was still ignoring it?

'Of course you don't,' GR says soothingly, then he adds, with just a hint of a quirk, 'But you will, because otherwise you won't know what might be going on and it'll drive you mad.'

He *can't* know me that well in such a short time! I wail to myself, while delivering a really good glare in his direction.

So we all go out to the property on Saturday morning, and GR takes Alex on a tour. As I haven't seen much more than the lily pool, I tag along in the back seat of the vehicle. Which also gives me a chance to gaze longingly at the back of GR's head.

Love is really strange, isn't it? That even the back of a perfectly normal head could be the focus of such attention?

We return a little after two, and Elizabeth feeds us a magnificent—if slightly late—lunch, after which the older members of the party retire to squatters' chairs on the veranda.

'Come for a ride, Blue?'

GR's frowning, though he must know I'll say yes. I told him last time how much I missed riding.

We head off in a different direction to the one we took last time, but eventually end up at the same pool. The sun's sinking behind low mountains to the west and the vivid purple and orange of the sunset is reflected in the water.

We dismount for the horses to have a drink, then tie them up and sit down on the grass, hands linked around our knees. I want him so badly I feel as if I'm on fire, but there's so much unresolved.

My mother ran from the man she loved, sacrificing herself for him. I don't think I'm that noble—in fact, I know I'm not—but Alex loved my mother and how GR feels is a mystery.

'I spoke to Alex yesterday afternoon, and I think we've worked things out.' GR breaks the silence. He's not touching me but I can feel the shimmery heat our bodies generate vibrating in the air between us.

But his statement is confusing so I can't let myself be distracted by shimmery heat.

'What kind of things did you have to work out with Alex?' I ask, genuinely puzzled.

GR turns to me and smiles.

'Practical things, Blue,' he says gently, and he leans forward and kisses me on the lips. 'Like how you can get to know him better without going back with him now, and when we can both get away to Argentina so you can see whatever it is you're likely to inherit and decide what you want to do about it.'

He touches my hair, my cheek and draws a finger about the line of my lips. 'I was wrong to think you could do all that on your own.'

I must be frowning really ferociously because his finger now moves to smooth away my frown lines. I'm going to need so much botox I should consider changing specialties.

'What are you talking about?' I demand. 'Why should *we* both go to Argentina?'

He smiles and kisses me again.

'Because you don't want to be separated from me. You said so yourself. And when I thought about it, I realised I didn't want to be separated from you either, so I took things from there. Alex will go home in a week or so, fix up his business matters, then come back and stay for six weeks out here on the property. That way he'll have something to do—he's really keen to see how we do things here and he'll probably go back up to Rosebud as well—and you'll be able to spend time with him. Then, when you finish your six months, I'll get a couple of months' leave and we'll both go to Argentina.'

If you think this is easing the frown lines, you're wrong. I'm frowning even more now, trying to make sense of all this. I replay the conversation in my head and pick on the most confusing bit of it.

'You don't want to be separated from me?' I repeat, turning so I can see the smallest glimmer of reaction. 'Why?'

He smiles and his eyes twinkle, and my heart dances in my chest, causing such a commotion I forget to breathe.

'Because I love you, Hillary Green. I thought you'd know that.'

'How?' I demand. 'By mental telepathy? You might be able to read my thoughts, but I've never been able to get inside your head.'

I would probably continue this aggrieved conversation, but he kisses me. Once he has me too breathless to speak, he draws away, stroking his knuckles down my cheek, watching my face—even blushing slightly—as he speaks.

'I haven't said it? Told you how much I've come to care for you? How much I long to see you every morning, to hear your voice and see your eyes flash when I aggravate you? I love you, Hillary, so deeply it terrifies me at times, while at others I feel I want to leap about and shout your name.'

GR leaping and shouting? I'm momentarily distracted, then he breathes my name a second time, a tender, whispered, love-impassioned, 'Hillary!

'See, I can use your name. No more distancing myself from you, though I think I'll always call you Blue, because that's how I think of you in my heart.'

The words are husky with emotion and brush shivers down my spine. He draws me close, kisses me again, murmurs more of love and loving, then shows me how he feels.

'It's funny,' he says later, now the stars are out above us—diamond bright in a velvet sky. 'I'd believed in love for a long time, but always thought it would come like friendship does, slowly building like the first flicker of a campfire until it became a source of all-over warmth.'

He gathers me in his arms again, kisses me, then adds, 'I didn't expect a comet—zooming into my life, sending heat and vibrations through the air. It wasn't the gentle flicker of a match set to a campfire but a conflagration, Blue, and every human instinct warned me to stand back. But I couldn't resist the comet's lure. I love you!'

We do go back to the homestead at some time that night, but not to sleep in separate beds. It's time everyone knew about our love. But love doesn't stop you worrying, I discover. In fact, I have more to worry about now. Curled up beside the warm body of the man I'm going to marry, I start to worry about our children if I keep working for him as his partner. I wouldn't want both of us in the same small plane, you see, in case it crashed and the children became orphans.

Of course, if I give up work altogether, GR's won the argument about women doing O and G then dropping out, so that's impossible.

'Bilbarra and the surrounding district is large enough to expand the private practice,' a deep voice says.

I peer through the darkness as Gregor moves and props himself against the pillows, pulling me close so my head is on his chest.

'What are you talking about?' I demand, certain he can't read my mind when he's asleep.

'Your future as a specialist,' he says, and though it's dark I know he's smiling. 'I know you're worrying about it, and you're too good at what you do to stop practising, so when we have a family you can take over the private practice here in Bilbarra—do a couple of days a week—and I'll stay on as the FOG.'

OK, so he *can* read my mind while he's asleep.

But can he read my next thought?

'With one proviso,' I tell him, and wait.

He kisses me, a long, smoochy kiss.

'As long as the department only sends male registrars?' he guesses, and we both laugh.

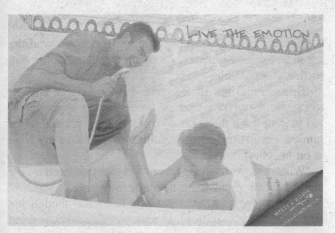

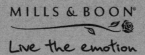

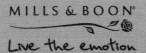

MILLS & BOON®

Live the emotion

Medical Romance™

SURGEON IN CRISIS by *Jennifer Taylor*

A posting to Mexico with Worlds Together was going to be an adventure for Sister Rachel Hart. And when she met the medical aid organisation's founder and surgeon, Shiloh Smith, her heart really started to pound. But Shiloh was a widower, and didn't believe that special love came more than once for anyone...

THE POLICE SURGEON'S RESCUE
by *Abigail Gordon*

Working for GP and police surgeon Dr Blake Pemberton is as close a brush with the law as Nurse Helena Harris wants. But then she finds herself testifying against a gang who threatened her father's life. Blake is determined to protect Helena, and she soon finds herself falling for this very courageous doctor...

THE HEART CONSULTANT'S LOVER
by *Kate Hardy*

Miranda Turner gave up on love a long time ago. Now she's wedded to her career – and her prestigious new job as consultant in cardiology. Senior Registrar Jack Sawyer is furious at Miranda's appointment. He wants to hate her, but can't help respecting her. And soon their powerful attraction explodes into a steamy affair!

On sale 2nd April 2004

Available at most branches of WHSmith, Tesco, Martins, Borders, Eason, Sainsbury's and all good paperback bookshops.

0304/03b

0404/108/MB95

FREE
4 BOOKS
AND A SURPRISE GIFT!

We would like to take this opportunity to thank you for reading this Mills & Boon® book by offering you the chance to take FOUR more specially selected titles from the Medical Romance™ series absolutely FREE! We're also making this offer to introduce you to the benefits of the Reader Service™ —

- ★ FREE home delivery
- ★ FREE monthly Newsletter
- ★ FREE gifts and competitions
- ★ Exclusive Reader Service discount
- ★ Books available before they're in the shops

Accepting these FREE books and gift places you under no obligation to buy; you may cancel at any time, even after receiving your free shipment. Simply complete your details below and return the entire page to the address below. *You don't even need a stamp!*

YES! Please send me 4 free Medical Romance books and a surprise gift. I understand that unless you hear from me, I will receive 6 superb new titles every month for just £2.69 each, postage and packing free. I am under no obligation to purchase any books and may cancel my subscription at any time. The free books and gift will be mine to keep in any case.

M4ZEF

Ms/Mrs/Miss/Mr ....Initials ....
BLOCK CAPITALS PLEASE

Surname ....

Address ....

....

....Postcode ....

Send this whole page to:
UK: FREEPOST CN81, Croydon, CR9 3WZ
EIRE: PO Box 4546, Kilcock, County Kildare (stamp required)